An Outlaw Entitlement
Short Story Anthology
Volume 1
Published by

WhirlWhirl Publishing

Copyright © 2022

Cover designs by David J. Knight
Book design by V.R. Leavitt
Published by WhirlWhirl Publishing
www.whirlwhirl.com[1]

---

1.   http://www.whirlwhirl.com

Table of Contents

Introduction

Dear Brave Soul,

Hello. My name is Chris, but my friends call me Outlaw. You should stick with Chris. It's not like we're dating. I was born on the first Wednesday of November, 1975 on the Gregorian calendar and according to the paper placemats at American "Chinese" restaurants, I'm a rabbit. Then, I decided to publish an anthology of short stories.

Should you ever find yourself deciding to publish an anthology of short stories, you'll likewise find that you have many questions for yourself. Do I need a publisher? Will anyone actually read my anthology? Who will I invite to participate? Will my anthology have a theme, or themes? Why am I talking to myself?

Let me attempt to reveal some of the answers to these questions. It should be noted that my answers will only address the issues from my perspective. Furthermore, I shall address them in a thoroughly postmodern way.

I wrestled with myself for a while over whether I would try to work with a publisher or if I'd just self-publish. To me it seems that people try to work with a publisher for three reasons: they want the professional help that can be provided by a publisher such as editing and compiling, they want the publisher to use its resources to sell their book, and/or they seek the sense of validation that comes from being selected by the publisher.

Let's start at the tail of this dragon and eat our way towards the head. Most of us are insecure and seek validation, and having a recognized publisher buy the rights to our books provides a sense of accomplishment and success. We feel that anyone can self-publish, but my book is so good that someone with an MFA who works for a publishing house that was probably inherited by its current owner loves my book so much that she's willing to risk her job and the owner's un-hard-earned money on it. Fortunately, as an American white male I have a sense of entitlement that renders me immune to the need of such approval.

Sales are a different matter. My plan when I started walking this lemming 5K was that everyone involved with the anthology would sell at least one copy to a family-member. So, we'd sell around 12 copies. I could use some mild assistance with sales.

Did you notice the "postmodern" that I slipped in a few paragraphs back? Of course, you did. There's very little chance that you didn't find yourself thinking just what does he mean by that? It's okay if you don't know. You're fine. I don't know, either. No one knows what "postmodern" means.

I need so much help with editing. As you're sitting there having serious buyer's remorse over the purchase of this book, the spelling and grammar checker that I'm using currently has my digital musings underlined in three different colors. That and the fact that I don't even know what compiling means point to a strong need for me to either learn how to do these things on my own or get some publishing assistance.

The universe provided WhirlWhirl. WhirlWhirl is a publishing venture started by an old friend and a soon to be new friend. Their info is in the frontmatter of the book. So, I shan't bug you with details. Their desire for contributors and my need of publishing assistance just happened to meet on the dance floor with the right song playing when we were all wearing equally suggestive clothing. Yadda yadda yadda, we're having a project-baby.

"Postmodern" has truly become nothing more than a loyalty oath. Conservatives seem convinced anything postmodern is just reverse racism, which isn't their brand, and progressives won't do anything that doesn't swear to be 10% more postmodern than whatever the center-left is totally being status quo about.

The project itself is my attempt to draw together a collection of a visual artist, a handful of authors, and a smattering of fairly obvious pen names on a common theme. The trick is coming up with a theme that won't cramp the various artists' styles.

Each artist is allowed to produce in any genre they should desire. In fact, I would prefer as much stylistic diversity as possible. There is only one catch: every contributor is required to produce an entry for a shared title that I provide. So, every story and the cover art all have the same title.

Hence, my entitlement is all around. That entitlement includes my entitlement as giver of the title, and my entitlement as not needing permission to launch this project. 'See how clever I am?

The artists who were invited were genuinely thrilled by the idea. Some of their excitement wavered a bit when I gave them *Nose Candy* for a title. I, on the other hand, had faith in the title and in the artists themselves. *Nose Candy*, as a title, had legs. I knew that the artists would have fun with it, and they all more than proved me right by their fine works.

Please, don't message me to explain postmodernism to me. It's just a joke. Let it go.

Of course, my runaway sense of entitlement wasn't enough to finish this project. Even the start was a bit rough given my numerous and foolish mistakes. I won't list them all, but at one point it had to be pointed out to me that I hadn't even set a word count. I corrected that mistake by setting a word count that would have excluded many of the greatest short stories ever written, but my next word count was solid.

This project would be nowhere without the grace and talent of its contributors and their patience with me.

You have already witnessed the cover of this book. So, you've seen the first artist's *Nose Candy*. I, now, invite you to enjoy the rest.

Postmodernly yours,
Christopher B. Outlaw
Managing Editor

Nose Candy

Lucy Waterson

• • • •

"YOU KNOW WHAT THEY'RE doing, don't you?" Cade muttered sourly, as he followed Raoul along the narrow street.

Raoul stopped so abruptly that Cade collided with his back and stumbled into the road.

"First of all," Raoul said, turning to face his friend. "No, I don't know, and second of all, who are they?"

"They." Cade waved his arms in the air and Raoul ducked.

"You mean Commander Blankinsop?"

"Oh naturally you and Blankinsop are on first name terms."

Raoul looked at Cade and then, unable to help himself, laughed. "You do realise Commander isn't actually his first name?"

"Never said I did," Cade sneered. "Probably doesn't have one."

"Doesn't have what?"

"A first name."

Raoul shook his head. "Maybe we should focus," he suggested. "Captain Talbot said she was found at the end of this street."

"Not very nice is it?" Cade said, as they started walking again. "Dying on the street, just so much trash."

"I suppose you want to die in your own bed, surrounded by grandchildren."

"Either that or blown sky high." Cade grinned. "Can you smell something?"

Raoul was just about to comment that he'd had a bath only two nights ago when he realised he too could smell something.

It wasn't just the scent of a dead body. Both constables knew that smell, you didn't get to be in the Watch for very long without encountering the stench of death. There was an overpoweringly sweet odour in the air. The type of smell that catches you at the back of the throat.

"Hey." Cade caught hold of Raoul's arm and pointed out into the road. "Looks like we've found her."

The woman's body was just visible from where Raoul and Cade were standing. They could see that her arms were stretched up above her head. Mounded around her and scattered across her face were a multitude of flowers. Raoul bent and picked one up.

"Sweet peas." He looked at Cade.

"Sweet peas?"

"It's the name of this particular type of flower."

Cade grinned. "I suppose it makes sense that a Citizen would know all the different types of flower."

Raoul let the blossom fall from his hand. "I don't know all of them."

"That's all right then. I'd hate to think I'd been partnered with a flower expert."

Raoul scowled. "How about we focus, huh?"

Cade crouched down next to the body. "Why cover her in flowers?"

Raoul took up a position next to Cade. He reached out and brushed pink and purple petals from the woman's hair. "She is a flower seller."

"She was stabbed." Gingerly Cade lifted the woman's jacket away from her body. The wound in her stomach was small, but the edges were ragged, as though her assailant had twisted the knife in the wound. "Whoever it was, he wasn't very happy."

"That's an understatement." Raoul stood up.

Cade stood too. "Unhappy customer?" He shrugged.

"What about witnesses?"

"I don't think she was killed here, not enough blood and the air's all wrong."

"Air?" Even after a year partnered with Cade, Raoul still wasn't used to the fact that his friend could sense things that weren't immediately obvious to other people.

"Too still, too calm." Cade looked at Raoul, frustration evident on his face. "So, what now?"

"Wait for the surgeon to come and collect the body."

"And in the meantime I'll go knock on a few doors. Maybe someone saw something."

Standing guard by a dead body wasn't Raoul's idea of fun, but he knew that Cade would likely get a better response from the people he spoke to. The man had a natural charm which people seemed to respond to. Raoul looked down at the woman wondering again why anyone would have wanted to kill her. The scent of the sweet peas seemed to be intensifying and Raoul rubbed a hand across his nose. He would likely be smelling them in his sleep.

. . . .

"ESME CARTER." CADE presented the name with a slight flourish. "She's been selling flowers here for the last five years, except not yesterday. Oh, and do you want to know something interesting?"

Raoul rolled his eyes. "Just get to the point."

"She didn't sell sweet peas."

"Anything else?"

"Surgeon'll be here soon. I heard his wagon clattering along two streets away."

Once the surgeon had taken the body Cade stretched and yawned. "Back to the Watch House?" he suggested. "I'm dying for a cup of tea and a bacon sarnie."

Raoul stood and looked at the heaps of flowers. "You don't think we should clear all of these up, do you?"

Cade shook his head. "Leave 'em. Bloody Scavengers will be along as soon as we leave. They're probably already watching."

Raoul looked up and glanced around, his eyes bright. "Really? Where do you think they are? I'd really like to meet a Scavenger."

Cade pulled the cap on his head straight and dusted a few petals from his jacket. "You really don't."

"What will they do with the flowers?"

Cade shrugged. "No idea. Maybe they'll eat them. With Scavengers, who knows? C'mon, let's get out of here."

• • • •

THE RETURN TO THE WATCH House meant that a report needed to be written. After watching Cade labour over a piece of paper, Raoul stretched out a hand and snagged it over to his side of the table.

"Let me do it. Otherwise we'll be here all night."

For once Cade didn't say anything, no snide comments about Raoul's education or background. *Probably worried if he says anything I'll change my mind.* Raoul dipped his pen into the inkwell and began to write. The scritch scratch noise of the nib against the paper made him smile.

"Here." Cade shoved a sketch across the table at Raoul. "How accurate would you say that was?"

Raoul looked down at the page and sucked in a breath. Cade might struggle when it came to writing up a report but his artistic talent was astonishing.

"That's exactly how it was."

"And just in time," Cade drawled, as he shoved his chair back from the table, and stood up. "Captain."

With a glare directed at Cade for the lack of warning, Raoul bounced to his feet.

"You boys had time to write up your report yet?" Unlike some of the other officers Captain Talbot didn't stand on ceremony, one of the reasons why all the new constables wanted to work with him.

"We've just finished."

"Good. Initial thoughts?"

"Whoever killed her obviously has a thing for flowers. But no one saw anything so unless the murderer has an attack of conscience and stumbles into the Watch House to confess I'm not sure what else we can do," Raoul said and looked at Cade.

"Uh... yeah... what he said."

Captain Talbot nodded, brown eyes intent on the two constables for a moment. "All right." He sighed. "I really hate to let cases like this one go."

Raoul and Cade exchanged glances, but neither man said anything.

. . . .

THE NEXT DAY WAS THEIR day off. It was nice, Raoul reflected, not to have a day when they had to shovel their breakfasts down as fast as possible so they could go out on patrol.

"Hey, Raoul."

The red haired man looked up. It was Ned, cheeks flushed and breathing hard as though he'd been running.

"Cade." The young man leant over, hands on knees, while he tried to catch his breath.

The two constables looked at each other and Cade took a bite out of his piece of toast.

"Captain Talbot sent me, he says could you please report to his office as soon as possible."

"It's our day off," Cade said with a scowl. "Why does he want us?"

"He said to tell you there's been another one."

"Bloody hell," Cade complained, as he sent his chair rocketing backwards away from the table.

. . . .

ANOTHER DEAD FLOWER seller, although in a completely different part of the city. The only good thing about it was that they had to take a cab to get there.

Cade always found the clopping of horses' hooves soporific, and he could feel his eyes falling closed as the cab rumbled through the streets.

"Wake up, sleepyhead." Raoul's elbow connected with his ribs, and Cade jerked awake.

"You want the other end of the street," the cab driver told them as the two constables jumped down onto the road. The horse tossed its head and Cade backed away, just a few steps, he didn't like horses. "I'll wait here for you if you like."

Moving off down the street Cade glanced back at the cabby. "Bet this is a great day out for him. Nothing to do but sit back and read the newspaper."

Raoul, several strides ahead of Cade, didn't say anything, and Cade hurried to catch up with him.

"It's our day off," Cade grumbled.

"Maybe you should have told Captain Talbot that."

"I tried," Cade pointed out. "You stopped me."

"You can say thank you later. You know the captain doesn't like shirkers."

"It's hardly shirking when it's our one bloody day off." Cade lengthened his stride so that he passed Raoul. "Gods, there's that smell again."

"Not quite," Raoul said, gesturing to where a sweep of purple flowers were taking up a large part of the road. "Different flower. Lavender this time."

"Right." The flowers crushed by his boots were letting off a very pungent scent and for a moment Cade's head swam, it was so strong. "Looks a bit older than the last one," he commented. The woman's head had been left free of flowers and there were wrinkles on her cheeks and white hair at her temples.

"Still just as dead." Raoul reached out to close the woman's eyes.

Cade stepped away from the body. "Same killer?"

"Maybe." Raoul sounded cautious.

Cade crouched down at the edge of the carpet of flowers and wrinkled his nose. "Some of these are soaked in blood."

"So she was killed here?"

"The scent's so strong I can't be sure, but I think so."

"And what's the betting she didn't sell lavender?"

Cade straightened up and stretched out his back. "What do you reckon?" He waved his hand towards where a small group of bystanders were watching. "Worth talking to?"

Raoul shrugged. "Possibly, although I can't imagine any of them saw anything."

There were four people watching from a distance, three women and a man. All of them stared as Cade walked towards them and the constable, remembering the lessons on how to walk with authority, took measured strides.

"Did you know...um... the deceased?" Cade was unsure which word he should use to cause the least offence. He tipped the brim of his cap back so he could get a proper look at the faces fixed on him.

"I did," the oldest of the women said after a short pause. "I live just around the corner."

"And did she work here every day?"

"Not in the winter or when the weather was bad, but other than that, yes."

One of the younger women had eyes that were wide with shock.

"Did you know her, miss?"

"No. I just came here to buy flowers. I'm getting married and one of my friends told me I should see Lila."

Well at least you'll have an interesting story to tell your guests. That was what Cade wanted to say but he restrained himself.

"What about you, sir?" Cade had noticed that the man had not taken his eyes off the woman's body.

With what Cade thought was obvious reluctance the man focused on Cade.

"Me, no." He glanced at the older woman and a frown creased his face. "But I did buy some flowers from her just yesterday."

"What sort of flowers?"

"Roses, for my fiancée. Everyone says Lila sells the best roses. Nose candy, she calls them."

"She, sir?"

"My finacée Clarissa."

Cade made a note with a stub of a pencil and frowned. "Received well were they, sir?"

"Yes." The man smiled. "I only wish I'd bought them for her sooner. I had hoped to get some more today."

"Plenty more flower sellers in the city," Cade said, noting the look the man gave him in response to his comment.

Knowing that Captain Talbot would complain otherwise Cade dutifully recorded names and addresses in his notebook. Then he ambled back to Raoul.

Raoul gave him a look.

"I don't know," Cade said. "She certainly was killed here, but the smell, it's making me dizzy."

Other than making a sketch of the scene, there wasn't much more they could do.

• • • •

"LILA DEAN," CADE LATER told Captain Talbot, glancing at Raoul as he did so. "She'd been selling flowers on that street corner for twenty years. Before that she was at Kings Street."

"Thank you, Constable." Talbot was looking thoughtful, never a good sign.

"You think the two murders are connected?" Cade couldn't stop himself from asking.

Talbot sighed and ran a hand over his stubble. The captain never seemed to be clean shaven, even though all members of the Watch were required by regulation to shave.

"I hope not. Otherwise we've got some mad man out there picking off flower sellers one by one. Can you say the words *panic in the streets*, Constable?"

Captain Talbot had just opened his mouth to say something else when another constable pushed his way through the door.

"Sorry, sir." The young man had flushed bright red. "I was told to give you this urgently." He handed across a piece of paper and the frown on Talbot's face deepened considerably as he read.

"Who brought this in?" Talbot fixed the constable in place with a stare.

"One of the southern runners," the constable said.

"All right." Talbot laid the paper down on his desk and Cade had the uneasy feeling that he and Raoul were not going to get to enjoy the rest of their day off after all.

Talbot sent the constable away and then he beckoned Raoul and Cade closer and indicated they should sit down.

"Another murder?" Cade asked.

Captains normally didn't like it when the lower ranks spoke out of turn, and so perhaps it was a sign of how stressed Talbot was that, rather than objecting to Cade's question, the man merely nodded.

Talbot's brow furrowed with thought and the man ran his hands through his grizzled hair. "Three flower sellers in two days." Talbot glanced from Raoul to Cade. "That's practically an epidemic."

Cade looked at Raoul and arched an eyebrow.

"Could we see the crime scene report please, sir?"

"Here." Talbot handed the paper over. "Perhaps you can spot a solution because I'm damned if I can."

Cade leant over Raoul's shoulder. He couldn't read as fast as his friend so he muttered his thanks when Raoul pushed the paper across so he could read it properly.

"Killed on the street corner where she plied her trade."

"And found surrounded by roses." Cade plonked a finger down onto the page to remind himself where he had got to, and looked at Talbot. "Whoever the killer is they would seem to have access to large quantities of flowers."

"Another flower seller?" Raoul suggested. "Trying to do away with the competition?"

"Or someone who grows flowers for a living. How do you boys feel about a field trip?"

• • • •

"WELL, THAT WENT WELL," Cade said, as he followed Raoul back into the room they shared. "So not only do we not get our day off but we have to drive across half of Anwich to talk to people who spend their lives growing flowers."

"You don't sound very happy."

"I didn't join the Watch so I could interview farmers, that's all."

• • • •

ONCE THEY WERE CLEAR of the outskirts of Anwich the air suddenly became a lot fresher and Raoul breathed deeply.

"This is better, isn't it, Cade?" Raoul nudged his friend, but the only response he got was a scowl.

The two constables had been dropped off at the edge of the farm. Behind them the road stretched back to where Anwich skulked on the plain like some vast sleeping beast. In front of them a variety of brightly coloured fields stretched out to the horizon.

Cade stamped his feet on the road. "I don't see how being here is doing any good," he complained. "We ought to be in the city, keeping an eye on the flower sellers."

Raoul shook his head. "Do you have any idea how many flower sellers there are in Anwich?"

Cade shrugged and took the cap off his head. "Ten maybe, twenty?"

"I don't know the exact number," Raoul admitted and Cade laughed. "But I'm guessing it's more than you and I can keep track of."

"There are a lot of other constables in the Watch," Cade said as they started walking. "One constable or two maybe to each flower seller, sorted."

"I can see the powers that be loving that suggestion. Better to concentrate on catching the killer."

"Rather than protecting the potential victims, you mean?" Cade lengthened his stride a little so he was walking just ahead of Raoul. "Spoken like a true Citizen, mate. Eye on the bottom line as always."

"Hey." Raoul broke into a jog. "I'm with you on this one. Let's get our job done here and then we might be able to stop any more killings."

Cade shrugged off the argument as easily as he might have shrugged off his coat. "Look." He gestured towards a man who was hurrying towards them. He was short and bald, his shirt untucked, and his trousers were covered in mud. "I'm guessing that's the owner."

"Carson Brightwell, Constables. I understand you want to talk to me."

"That's right." Raoul said.

"We should talk in my office then. We'll be more comfortable there."

As Brightwell led them towards a rather dilapidated house, the man kept up a stream of chatter.

"Most of the flowers we grow here are sold in Anwich. You city people sure do like your blooms. Heavily scented varieties mostly.

Lavender's the easiest to grow, but roses are popular too, so yes we sell a lot of roses. Flower growing season's actually pretty good, and in the years we get a warm autumn we can get even more grown. O'course a warm autumn is often followed by a particularly harsh winter, but that can be good for the soil, so it all balances out in the end."

"How do you manage during the winter?" Cade asked when Brightwell finally fell silent. "No fresh flowers during the winter."

"Very true." Brightwell gestured past the house they were approaching, towards a long low barn some distance away. "That there is our preserving shed. We dry the flowers in there and that's our winter income." Brightwell grinned. "Ah, here we are. Come inside. I expect you'd like some refreshments."

Brightwell's office was located on the ground floor of the building. A large window overlooked one of the fields where lavender was growing. The flowers made a carpet of purple and Cade was glad that the window was shut since the smell would no doubt be overwhelming.

Brightwell smiled. "Make yourselves comfortable while I go and see about some tea."

Cade didn't look around the room properly until Brightwell had gone, then he wandered across to the opposite wall which was covered in book shelves.

"Who would have thought there were so many books about growing flowers?"

Raoul, who was standing gazing out of the window, turned to look at his friend. "It's so peaceful here."

"Peaceful?" Cade gave a mock shudder. "Quiet as the grave is what it is. Give me Anwich any day."

"City boy," Raoul said with a grin.

"You know," Cade said, carefully replacing a book that he had been flicking through, "that insult would work a lot better if you hadn't grown up in Anwich as well."

Raoul shrugged and laughed. "You've got a point. So, do you think Brightwell's a viable suspect?"

"Ole mister flower power?" Cade shook his head. "I'd be surprised if he ever made it past the outskirts. Information only."

Any further conversation was halted when Brightwell backed his way into the room. He was carrying a large tea tray and Raoul hurried forward to help him. Cade remained by the wall of books, watching Brightwell. So far the man seemed genuine enough. He was clumsy too, knocking the cups over as he reached for the teapot and then somehow managing to pour tea onto the desk rather than into the cup he had been aiming for. Cade tried to picture him sneaking up on a woman and then violently stabbing her, and he just couldn't do it. He altered the scenario in his head, trying to get a clear picture of what might have happened. It was a knack he had although it didn't always work, like now when he couldn't get the picture to coalesce properly. He saw Raoul watching him and he shook his head.

"Why don't I pour, Mister Brightwell." Raoul picked up the teapot and expertly poured three cups. So expertly he might have been trained to do it, which, knowing Raoul's mother, he probably had been.

A look of relief spread across Brightwell's face and he plonked himself down into a chair. Raoul handed the man a cup, gave one to Cade, and then gestured towards the view.

"That's quite a sight. You must be the major supplier of the Anwich flower trade."

Brightwell sipped his tea and nodded. "Yes indeed. My family have been growing flowers here for the past three generations. Everything we grow goes to Anwich."

"Everything?" Cade asked, deliberately making his tone disbelieving.

"Everything that matters," Brightwell said, going a little red in the face.

Cade looked over at Raoul and raised an eyebrow.

"And what sort of flowers do you grow?" Raoul asked.

"Lavender clearly," the man said, gesturing towards the window. "Roses, particularly the ones with a nice strong scent to them."

"What about sweet peas?" Cade asked. "Do you grow any of those?"

"On and off," Brightwell admitted. "They're quite frail little flowers and not as popular either. Although." And here Brightwell stopped to frown. "I have heard there is beginning to be an increasing demand for them."

"Oh?"

"Well they're very pretty, and I believe there's a fashion now for wearing posies of flowers attached to one's clothing."

"Believe?"

Brightwell put his cup down onto the desk, his hands shook. Although that could merely be nervousness from being questioned. "I never venture into Anwich, Constable."

He'd been right, so at least he could take satisfaction in that.

Raoul looked down at his notebook and ran a finger along under something he had written. It was for show only, a little performance that Raoul quite enjoyed and Cade thought was unnecessary. The general public already thought the Watch was full of uneducated louts, there was no need to emphasise the point.

"You said," Raoul said, looking up at Brightwell before glancing back at his notepad. "That everything you grow here ends up in Anwich."

Brightwell raised a finger. "Almost everything."

"Almost everything," Raoul repeated, picking up his pencil and making a show of amending his notes. "You have the monopoly?"

Brightwell shook his head with a rueful smile. "I wish."

"There are other flower farmers?"

"Not many," Brightwell admitted. "Farmers are largely supposed to concentrate on food production."

"But not you?"

"As I said my family have been here for three generations. As you can see," the man said, pointing to a small white and gold certificate hanging in a frame on the wall. "We operate under royal appointment."

Cade looked at Raoul. "So how many others are there?"

"Aside from us, one other."

"Near here is it?" Cade asked, wondering if they might be able to visit the second farm on their way back to the city.

"No. The owner's a man by the name of Gentry."

"First name? Last name?" Raoul's pencil was once more poised to write.

"Only name I think. 'Sides, I've never heard him referred to by any other name. His farm used to be scrubland. Word is it took him years to get it fertile."

"So, you're rivals?"

Brightwell looked uncomfortable. "I wouldn't go that far. I do know he's been angling to get his flowers onto Anwich's streets."

"Tough thing to do, huh?"

"Constable, the desire for fresh flowers in Anwich is still relatively new. It used to be that the main demand was from Citizen house-keepers looking for ways to sweeten the home environment. Hence the lavender and the roses. But, as I already told you, fashions are changing."

"Tell that to the Watch," Cade muttered.

"I believe Gentry is attempting to cater for the new fashion."

"You're not tempted?"

Brightwell sounded affronted when he answered. "There will always be demand for the flowers that I grow."

"So where do we find this Gentry character then?"

"His farm is on the river side of the city, but he's never there. He's got a small house in Anwich, just outside the Citizens' Quarter."

"Of course he has." Cade quirked an eyebrow in Raoul's direction. "Back to Anwich we go."

• • • •

AS THE CARRIAGE JOSTLED and rolled around them Cade yawned and, in the absence of other passengers, he propped his feet up on the seat opposite.

"Likely suspect?"

"Possibly." Raoul opened the window a little, he hated being confined in a carriage. "But I can't see what reason he'd have for killing flower sellers. Surely he would want more of them not less, and he didn't sound at all bothered by the fact that he has competition."

Cade shrugged. "Well, let's see what this Gentry has to say for himself. Funny sort of farmer though, if you ask me, one who lives in the city."

• • • •

GENTRY'S HOUSE WAS easy to find. It was located just outside the Citizens' Quarter in Offal Street, and Raoul, certain that Cade would grab at the opportunity to make a terrible joke, was almost disappointed when he didn't.

There had been a slaughterhouse here once, hence the street name, until population pressures had led some of the less wealthy Citizens to move outwards. The new neighbours had been incredibly affronted by the sounds of animal distress they found themselves listening to on a triweekly basis, even as they tucked into the carefully prepared meat on their dinner plates, and the slaughterhouse had been forced to close. The building had been converted into living accommodation. It was occupied mostly by misfits, although rumours were that at least one member of the Watch had rooms in the massive edifice.

Raoul, having grown up only a few streets away, knew the history but Cade proceeded smoothly along the street without showing any interest in his surroundings.

"It's this one." Raoul stopped and, grinning at Cade, he made a fist and banged on the door. "Anwich City Watch," he bellowed, ensuring that the whole street would hear.

The door was opened by a sharp nosed little man wearing what, Raoul thought, was an overly complicated waistcoat and a pair of old fashioned trousers.

"Mister Gentry," Raoul said. "My name's Constable Bettancourt of the Anwich City Watch. I wonder if I might come in and talk to you."

The little man pursed his lips but eventually he nodded and Raoul followed him into the house, Cade on his heels.

He led them into a narrow room which contained a winged back chair and nothing else. Glancing around Raoul decided the sparsity of the room was deliberate. Gentry was obviously used to keeping people at a distance.

The man sat himself in the chair and gazed at the two constables. He looked very unhappy. Raoul glanced at Cade, but Cade was frowning, his gaze fixed on Gentry.

"What do you want, Constable?"

Raoul gave a brief but succinct description of recent events. Despite Captain Talbot's best efforts a report on the first murder had appeared in this morning's newspaper and by the look of the man seated opposite Raoul would have been prepared to make a bet that Gentry didn't start his day until he had read at least one newspaper.

"Do you think I have something to do with it? I am merely a man trying to make his way in the world, just as many others do."

"And just how exactly do you make your way in the world?" Cade asked.

Gentry looked astonished and then affronted. Raoul, deciding that Cade wouldn't respond well to being looked at that way, asked another question.

"You own a farm, is that right?"

"I do have a small concern, yes. But I still fail to see how this relates to the murders you've described."

Cade growled, deep in his throat, and Gentry jumped. Raoul hid his smile.

"We're simply trying to build up a picture of how the buying and selling of flowers in Anwich works, Mister Gentry. As one of only two suppliers you would seem to be fairly important."

"Ah." Gentry steepled his fingers and what Raoul recognised as a very patronising smile slid across the man's face. "That of course presupposes that these murders have any connection to flowers. They may of course be totally unrelated."

Cade's laughter made Raoul jump.

"Why didn't we think of that? Flower sellers are being killed and their bodies left in the street surrounded by flowers, but of course it's probably nothing to do with flowers at all." Cade stepped forward and Gentry shrunk back into his chair. For a moment Raoul allowed himself to enjoy Cade's performance. His partner really did do aggression very well.

"Have you had any large orders recently?" Raoul asked, deliberately keeping his voice mild and unthreatening.

Gentry looked flustered. "I'm afraid I couldn't tell you offhand. I'm a very busy man and-"

"Yeah, we got that. But you've got records, you could check." Cade's tone made it clear he was not asking.

Raoul glanced back at Cade. "You need to back off a little, mate. Remember what happened last time?"

Cade snarled and Raoul took a careful step backwards. Gentry, looking concerned now, tracked his movements.

"Mister Gentry, perhaps you could check your records and then we'll be on our way," Raoul said, although his eyes remained locked on Cade.

"Of course." The little man sprang from his chair and hurried out of the room.

"So?"

Cade shook his head. "Nope. Besides Lila Dean put up one hell of a fight and I don't think he's strong enough."

"You say she fought back, and yet there are no witnesses, no one pulled aside their curtains to take a look."

Cade sniffed. "It's talk like that gives away the fact you're a Citizen. Where I grew up you hear a disturbance you take cover and hope nobody notices you."

"You're not picking up on anything?"

Cade scowled. "He beats his maid, other than that? Nothing."

Raoul was about to say something else, but Gentry chose that very moment to come back in.

"I did have a large order two weeks ago." Gentry suddenly seemed eager to please. "One thing that you gentlemen may not know is that traditional flower sellers only buy small quantities at a time. They have quite frankly very limited resources, and no means by which they can store the flowers."

"So who put in your order?"

Gentry beamed. "Oh, you'll like this, Constable. The order was made by Florence Carstairs to be delivered to an address in Welkin Street."

"You made the delivery?"

That question made Gentry puff up a little, like a startled cat. "Not personally, no. But the flowers she requested were delivered and paid for. Would you like me to write the name and address down for you, Constable?"

"No. No need for that."

• • • •

"YOU KNOW HER, DON'T you?" Cade said as he and Raoul made their way back to the Watch House.

"Yes, I know her." Raoul scowled. "She's number one on my mother's list of potential wives for yours truly."

"Wow." Cade patted Raoul on the shoulder. "You have my sympathy."

"Mother didn't mention anything about a flower shop." Raoul shrugged. "Probably because she doesn't approve."

"So are we going to see her?"

"Lunch first."

• • • •

ONE OF THE PROBLEMS with being a Watchman was that eating patterns could be erratic. Cade therefore was careful to always eat as much as he could whenever the opportunity arose.

So, it was with a very full stomach that Cade set off in the direction of Welkin Street. Raoul had managed to convince Captain Talbot that it would be better if Cade went without him. After all he was going to one of the most genteel parts of the city, how much trouble could he get into?

"Coward," Cade said as he pulled his cap on.

• • • •

WELKIN STREET WAS ONE of the shortest streets in the city and it wasn't hard for Cade to spot Florence's shop. There were pots brimming with flowers either side of the door, and Cade pressed his sleeve against his nose as he stepped across the threshold into the shop.

"Are you Florence Carstairs?" Cade asked as he spotted a woman arranging vases against a wall.

"That would be me." The woman was young, with thick blonde hair. Cade wasn't sure that he would describe her as pretty, but there was nothing unpleasant about her features.

"And you are?" The words were barbed and Cade, realising he had been staring, dropped his head and pretended to find his boots fascinating.

"Constable Hardy, Ma'am."

That made her giggle. "Ma'am?"

Cade grinned. "It's a nice little shop you have."

"Well I'm glad you think so. I'm not exactly overrun with customers though."

"No?" Cade feigned interest, turning to look at a tray brimming over with pink blooms. Raoul of course would have known exactly what they were.

"In Anwich change happens at a glacial speed, Constable. Most people are still content to buy their flowers from women standing on street corners. I'm just trying to move things on."

"By committing murder?"

Another giggle, before it sunk in that Cade was being serious and her eyes widened in shock.

"You think that was me?"

"Actually, no," Cade admitted unwillingly. "But it's possible that you've spoken to the murderer. He definitely seems to have a thing for flowers."

Florence looked shocked. As well she might, Cade thought, with a killer on the loose targeting flower sellers. Cade shook his head. She probably thinks she's safe, but a flower seller's a flower seller whether they're standing on a street corner or surrounded by four stone walls.

Cade looked around the shop. It was only small, but it was well stocked.

"Do you get a lot of customers?"

"A few." Florence inclined her head to one side, like a bird. "As I've already told you I'm having some difficulty persuading the people of Anwich that a shop is a perfectly pleasant place in which to buy flowers."

"Hmm." Cade pursed his lips and walked across to a large display of flowers. His nose itched. He was beginning to think he should have brought Raoul with him so that he wouldn't have to reveal how little he knew, but then he did spot a bloom he recognised.

"A rose." It was large and pink and Cade very gently touched the petals. "You've got so many different flowers here, but only one rose."

Florence smiled. "You like roses, Constable? Normally I would have more but I sold most of my stock yesterday."

"Sold?" The itch was turning into a tickle and Cade took a step backwards in case a sneeze was next.

"Yesterday. I sold almost all my roses to a male customer. Bless you."

"Thanks." Cade rubbed his nose on his coat sleeve. "Did he say what he wanted them for?"

"Something about a fiancée." Florence shook her head. "He did say something I thought was curious though."

"Oh?"

"He made a performance out of smelling all the flowers. He called them nose candy."

Cade smiled. "Thank you, miss. You've been very helpful."

· · · ·

"IT'S NOT A CRIME TO buy flowers, Constable."

"But two lots in three days?" Cade said. "Don't you think that's a bit excessive?"

Captain Talbot raised his eyebrows. "Neither is it a crime to buy a large amount of flowers."

"A bit odd maybe," Raoul said, and Cade twisted round to glare at him.

"But he bought flowers from Lila and he bought flowers from Florence. Don't you think we should at least try to find out if he bought flowers from the other dead women?"

"Miss Carstairs isn't dead," Captain Talbot pointed out.

"Yet." Cade looked the captain straight in the eye. "You know if we don't arrest Mister Barron and Florence ends up dead, you're gonna feel pretty bad."

Talbot's eyes were as hard as flints and Raoul nudged Cade hard with his elbow.

"That's no way to address a superior officer, Constable. I take it Miss Carstairs is pretty."

"I didn't really notice." Behind Cade, Raoul snorted. "Sir, please. Send me and Raoul. We'll watch the shop and if he tries anything we'll catch him."

"And meantime on the other side of the city some poor woman is left dead in the street surrounded by flowers."

"Won't happen."

. . . .

CROUCHED IN AN ALLEYWAY that reeked of urine and other things Raoul was very unhappy.

"Do you rank this as one of your better ideas, Cade?"

"Quiet, he'll hear you."

"There's nobody here but us and a few hundred rats." Raoul's legs were cramping and he really wanted to stand up and stretch.

"You sure about that?" Cade whispered directly into Raoul's ear. "Look."

Dusk was gathering and Raoul could see into the shop opposite. Florence was moving around inside, a watering can in one hand she was topping up the vases.

"Did you warn her?" Raoul asked.

"No." Cade recoiled from the look Raoul gave him. "She wouldn't have believed me. She has that supreme confidence thing that all you Citizens have."

"Not all of us."

Cade nudged Raoul and gestured towards the shadows. "See anything moving?"

Raoul couldn't see anything and he was just about to tell Cade that when he realised he *could* see movement.

A patch of deeper shadow coalesced somehow and a man stepped forward. He was bare headed, one hand tucked inside his coat, the other hand was stretched out towards the door.

Cade rubbed his nose. "It's him. Are you ready?"

"Yep."

The two men sprang from their hiding place.

"City Watch," Raoul bellowed as they ran, and that momentary distraction was enough to enable them to make it across the street with Cade grabbing at the outstretched arm and yanking it backwards, hard.

The man yelled out, pain mingled with surprise, and Cade pushed him to the ground. He was strong, surprisingly so, and it took both constables several minutes to subdue him. He rolled beneath them, muttering curses and Cade and Raoul rolled with him.

Eventually they managed to knock him out and both men sat back on their heels breathing hard.

• • • •

PERSONALLY CADE THOUGHT expecting them to write a report afterwards was a little too much. He sat and groused while Raoul did most of the hard work.

"His name is Noah Barron," Raoul told Captain Talbot. "He was trying to win over a Citizen woman by buying her flowers. She was, to put it as simply as possible, unimpressed, rejecting his efforts on several occasions. Barron blamed the flower sellers."

"Constable Hardy, would you like to add anything?"

"Other than that the man's psychotic? No, sir."

"All right." Captain Talbot settled back in his chair. "You didn't do too badly at all," he said with what Cade assumed was a smile. "Well done."

"That's it?" Cade complained, as soon as they were out of earshot of anyone else. "Well done. That's all we get?"

"Aside from the satisfaction of knowing that the city is now a safer place thanks to us, you mean?"

"Yes," Cade said. "That is the most important thing. Let's go get a beer."

Nose Candy

Andrew Benson Brown

There is a flower shop below my apartment. At all hours of the day and night, the perfumes of lavender, rose, freesia, eucalyptus and gardenia, honeysuckle and wisteria drift upstairs. The soft, sweet scents of peace and springtime. Most would think this merely a nice thing, a delicate and pale overlay to the ripe ambiance of urban living. But for me, nothing is pale. The result is intoxicating. I feel I have stepped out of time. A host of pleasant memories flash before me at once, the walls of my room recede, and I find myself standing at the nexus of eternity.

My neighbors do not see things under the aspect of eternity. They do not like me. The feeling is mutual. Attentiveness to truth always demands radical isolation. The sweat of crowds is ruinous to cognition; were I invited to a party, I would not accept. There would be no topics of common interest to sustain conversation if I did. The neighbors do not notice the flowers below them except on certain obligatory holidays. As soon as the roses wilt their message fades. Not so for one enduring an extreme sensitivity to smell: the rot of the rose is at least as worthy of beholding as its bloom. Like a person who, having undergone special eye surgery, can see the entire color spectrum and microscopic world, *hyperosmia* broadens the dimensions of the ephemeral. The consequence of this enlarged reality is that flowers are the only things worth talking about anymore.

Well, almost. There is also my work. You see, for the last seven years I have been writing a treatise on epistemology. There have been a few false starts along the way, a few annihilated manuscripts (the bleaching agents used in composition paper are nauseating to the creative process). I have since shifted methods. And I feel that *this time*, I will finish it. The mixed fragrances of chocolate and permanent marker are a continual stimulant to me as I jot my undying thoughts down on the thick paper backing of gold-foil Hershey's wrappers.

I have finally settled on a title. "Nose Candy: A Treatise on Olfactory Empiricism." Its basic purpose is to correct certain follies of Locke which have been hovering in the intellectual climate for centuries, misdirecting Western progress. Locke was, admittedly, right about most things: that we acquire knowledge through the senses is clear enough. But even the greatest philosophers are not without error. We can forgive Locke for this. After all, he was forced to induce British Empiricism from the smell of the British. The fog that hangs over London causes one's nose hairs to clump together; a person cannot see five feet ahead or discern the direction of hastening footsteps on the cobblestones. When one is engulfed in an epistemic mist, one must take particular care to parse complex ideas. A shame that the founders of the empirical method were not hyperosmiacs.

Allow me to summarize my fundamental axioms. They are so comprehensive that they can only be contained on the largest candy wrappers:

1. *Smell is the most important secondary quality.* It is mainly this capacity that produces ideas in our minds about the combinations of particles making up the texture, number, size, shape, and motion of things. Sugar may produce an idea of whiteness, yes, but its true nature is sweetness—among secondary qualities, vision is the most secondary. It is smell—SMELL!—which is the key to the primary qualities whose ideas resemble their causes. Insofar as color has any significance at all, it is the *scent and flavor* of color that resonate.

2. *The universe is comprised of odorants.* These particles of perception are all around us, floating between bodies, always in motion. They are all that exist. One cannot prevent inhaling

them. The smallest odorants of well-ground flour, though imperceptible to the eye, make their effect felt upon the nose and produce ideas in us; for example, that the baking of breads, cookies, and cakes should be a calm, controlled affair devoid of violent quarrels between envious chefs. Democritus's atoms are nothing but odorants, at bottom, and it was really these that soured the Persians to the Peloponnesian climate, causing them to fight badly on Greek shores. A quark, too, is nothing but a large odorant, and the nose needs no microscope to perceive it. Often have I tasted a sweet, pungent quark in the moments before a thunderstorm drips its heavenly nectar onto my waiting tongue.

3. *The nose is essential to cosmological order.* The understanding judges objects through it. Scent is the most elevated faculty of the soul—*and* the path to its deepest corruption. The progress towards knowledge is like panting up a mountain over a densely populated valley where smog hovers with the ozone; one must finely comb and trim (but never pluck) one's nasal hairs in order to distinguish the fresh air from the polluted.

4. *Deficiency in smell is a deficiency in mind.* Without smell, man's slate would remain blank. It connects all our ideas in agreement or disagreement. I say "our" ideas...but really I mean *my* ideas. For your ideas, dear reader, I am sorry to say are the products of crude and limited sensory perceptions. Most humans strain life through the eyeballs. For them, reality is a clogged sieve. Those who rely on vision are like blind men to the hyperosmiac, attuned to a lower sphere of reality where the dials have been turned down for easy listening (I mix my perceptual metaphors with intent). As soon as I discover something not to be true, I will turn up my nose at it. Other noses, though, are not so keen. Chained in an underground cave, they spend their lives smelling acrid guano; if a prisoner

is released, he will scramble outside to sniff the sunlight and attempt to describe its clean clear air to those below, who will not believe him, so absorbed are they in the falseness of the guano.

Not that the other senses are irrelevant, mind you. It is just that everything experienced by the eye, the ear, even the hands (and especially the tongue) are all filtered through the nose. I have heard the bowels of the sewer churning through grates blocks away, tasted barbeque in the mouth of a patron through a restaurant window, felt my pores absorbing the black fog of the skyscrapers. What is sour for most is like acid on my tongue; sweetness is an explosion of pleasure. Who needs heroin when you have peppermint candies?

For much of my youth, everything smelled red. Blood and lust, violence and strong passion were all. The scent of a passing woman made me fall madly in love with her, provided the perfume was not too cheap, and the sweat of the male hugging her shoulder would incite my aggressive instincts. The weak passions had no place in my habits. After several legal confrontations, experiences with baffled pedestrians from all walks of life led me to formulate the following, somewhat Berkleyan, axiom:

1. *The ideas of others, though not always entirely false, lack intensity and imagination.* Call these people what you will: sleepwalkers, zombies, children, idiots. With their faulty nasal cavities they cannot distinguish, compare, or abstract upon the nuances of baby powders or bed sheets, make trustworthy judgements about old paint, or verbalize the mysteries of the salty sea. The tangible scents inking my memory like fingerprints seem mere fancies to these boors drifting through a silent world. By the violence of my imagination I sometimes give the impression of being a madman, joining together wrong ideas and mistaking them for truths. Though sober

when it comes to other perceptions, smells make me frantic. I am fated to confront every object invisible to ordinary people of sub-comprehension. I can never say too much about odorants, but no amount of language can convey their obscure terrors.

It is dangerous for me to leave the city. More than once I have wandered through a half-domesticated wilderness while ruminating on the adjective 'woodsy,' attempting to disentangle and piece together the variegated aspects of its harmonious complexity, producing such extravagant chains of reasoning that I lose my path. The wondrous jumble of the damp grass, the hot afternoon air, the saps and resins of the pine, maple, and sumac; pollen floating with honeybees; mosquitos fat with the metallic blood types of campers; bug repellant brands and smoke of campfires; the berry-stained black bear chasing my fleeing, treat-filled backpack; the freshwater pool that invites my plunging gaze—it disorders my mind, it is all too much for me. When the park ranger resuscitates my purple face and I return home, I find my first principles of apartment-dwelling have been corrupted. Scarcely can I navigate the belly of the bathroom sink for a bar of soap to purify myself of Mother Nature's puddle-muddle. Serenity is full of hidden confusions under every rock and flower; I prefer the open confusion of urban holes and fissures.

One would think that living in a city is sensorily—and thus morally—corrupting to an olfactory empiricist. Exhaust fumes, overheating street lamps, fresh asphalt, broken plumbing. Fish markets. The swampy foundation under the concrete. The city is a web of clouds. But over the years I have trained myself to harness these stimuli to my benefit. Keeping them in balance is a form of continual meditation. I used to always keep my window closed to keep out the street. But now I have it open at all hours, no matter the weather. The city seeps into my being. *I am the city.*

My treatise would be ideally comprehensible when written in aromas rather than words, scratched on vellum with scented pigments by a monk reeking of incense and the musky shadow of divinity. But words are, alas, my only tools of communication, useful enough for getting where I need to be. Even the highest beings must compromise. Did not the Buddha, pure and without odor in heaven, descend from the fellowship of deities to enter into the "stinking abode of humans," as it says in the *Lalitavistara*? He had the benefit of being protected by chambers of sandalwood and perfume in his mother's womb. My own birth was the typical bloody affair of all animals. But through my divine capacity I imitate the sages.

I do not like dogs. Not because they are filthy creatures that consume their own fecal matter, but because when they wag their tails and sniff my groin they smell in me that which spread from Adam after his mortal sin, when he had already named each of the gathering beasts and the fragrances of Paradise were closed to him. Christ has yet to fulfill his promise to give back man's original cologne when he returns to us in robes scented with myrrh, aloe, and cassia; Calvin Klein strives in vain to recapture our Edenic essence. Of course, it was when Adam smelled the apple that the temptation was complete, smell being the father and king of taste. There was no need to bite into that waxy exterior to acquire a knowledge of good and evil. The beginning of man's fall into arrogance began with a hint of citrus and marzipan (if it was a Granny Smith), flowers and vanilla (Gala), or sugarcane (Golden Delicious—its blinding, blazing skin like the sun's corona). It is this primordial arrogance which a dog smells when we enter each other's ambit of olfactory influence.

An outlook as rigorously scientific as mine is not an excuse for debauched living. In fact, I am known to deny myself experiences that most deem pleasurable. Sometimes I will go to an expensive restaurant, order an unpronounceable dish, and position my face over the plate's rising steam when it arrives. There I will sit for a period, breathing in the shades of flavor and cleansing my pores. When it cools down, I complain to the waiter that it smells of food poisoning and leave without taking a bite to avoid paying. Tasting a gourmet meal is always anticlimactic. In my effort to acquire ultimate understanding nothing can corrupt the aromatic experience. This commitment is, in large measure, why I am wasting away. An Ear, Nose, and Throat Doctor once scribbled "eating disorder" in my chart, along with a list of improbable material causes for my divine capacity. But the medical establishment only recognizes that lower form of nutrition sucked in through the mouth. Olfactory empiricism is not a deviant health condition, however much this comprehensive worldview is applied to lifestyle.

Asceticism does not exclude aromatic indulgence. Indeed, some of the wildest aromatic hedonists I know are physical ascetics. In their *Saturnalia* of the spirit, scented candles are lit faster than wine goblets could be emptied at a feast—for a reveler is not confined to drinking one cup at a time. One nose is worth a hundred mouths. An ascetic with two nostrils is an orgy of sacrifice and grace, breathing incense clouds and smothering his frail bones with holy oils, intoxicated with blessedness. If only the oral epicurean knew what a crude being he is on the ladder of pleasures.

You may be curious as to how an olfactory empiricist can speak of spirit. For did I not say that all things are composed of odorants? And am I not now contradicting my apparent materialism? No, reader—for the spirit, too, is comprised of odorants. But where the rest of space is a mixture of odorants and void, the soul is a dense ball of pure odorants, refined to reflect every hue. Odorants are, in fact, the source of all light and the color spectrum. Each odorant is a God-particle. The nose is the window to the soul.

During the Apocalypse everyone, saved and unsaved alike, will contract hyperosmia. The Book of Revelations is quite clear on this point. Smell will be the first hint of a soul's redemption or damnation. In the latter case it will be quite horrible—the expected sulfur, the miasma of plague, black mold, skunk, and the rancid poetry of one's particular mortal sin. The scent of salvation will be familiar to those who have smelled a heavenly visitation or a dead saint's odor of sanctity: all the sweet notes of life will return in a culturally specific combination of sucralose, fried chicken, pipe tobacco, or whatever dinner and after-dinner habits the good believer followed.

My knowledge in this matter is due to personal contamination from sainthood. Call it a whiff of patrilineal expertise. My father was the unfortunate victim of an electric fire. At the moment of death his body warmed and expanded like baking bread, purifying like gold in a smelting furnace. The smoke from his flesh smelled of frankincense. While I was not present, I retroactively inducted this transformation of child abuser into an accidental martyr while spitting in his open coffin during the wake: as I sucked in my cheeks to gather a gob, I tasted particles of bliss in my saliva. It was an expansive flavor. This experience led to my next two axioms: 6. *There is in the mind an endless room for more smells.* The idea of infinity is derived from this. And from the idea of infinity, the conceptual leap to God is natural. God is That Being Than Which Nothing More Perfect Can Be Smelled. And what is this perfect smell, you ask? Simple. It is whiteness. This is not to say God is a sanitized blur of ammonia. Purity is an amalgam of every sweet element in creation—fruits, flowers, spices; among fauna: citronella ants, butter-popcorn bearcats, cucumbery copperheads, coriander bed bugs. Though He created all smells, He does not partake of the evil ones. He distills the sugar out of everything.

7. *Direct knowledge of God is derived from a functioning nasal passage.* Since I have the most high-functioning nasal passage on earth, it follows that, more than any other mortal, my experience and knowledge most closely approximate God's. Still, I fall far short of the Most Divine Nasal Passage. I have never smelled whiteness, being unable to filter out the savory and the pungent from my experience. When I come closest to smelling whiteness—when I am in Nature, standing

atop a mountain—the scent of sublimity overwhelms me even more than woodsiness.

My proper place is at sea level. Even at this common altitude I begin to feel one with creation.

Then something happened that changed everything: the barbeque restaurant below my apartment went out of business. Gone was the piquant sizzle of meat, the oak and maple wood chips, the sugary smoke lingering on my clothes. Suddenly, in its place, was a thrift store. Old clothes and vintage trinkets unleashed specters of decay around me, tormenting wraiths that floated between my mind and the world. The old woman who ran the store, a widower, stunk of the grave. In tune with the brown moths and cigarettes of the musty attic below, the bright crimson in my life dimmed, darkened. To garnet, merlot, mahogany. Then to black. The smell of death began to permeate me. I would strip and shower, add bleach to dark wash cycles. To no avail. I felt like an embalmed Pharaoh.

Early Christians knew that bad smells represented an evil inclination. The stench of illness, toilet water, and trash may indicate nearby demonic activity. I have always been suspicious of nurses, plumbers, and garbage collectors, but now I avoided them entirely. The overpowering sweetness of candy was revolting to me. Only the blandest food could be swallowed. The smell of fear on a pedestrian was contagious and every scent triggered a traumatic memory.

I stared at my nose in the mirror. For how long, I cannot say. It is not an elegant nose. Its bridge is wide and bumpy, its tip bulbous. Large and long, it disturbs the harmony of a face otherwise quite proportional and handsome. I dreamt of rhinoplasty and even made an appointment. But after my consultation I decided that a change in outward structure would not solve my inner problem.

I thought of lining up my fat despot against a wall like a firing squad and smashing it until my face was flat. But I lacked the courage. Instead, I began to wear a clothespin. To blot out the death and fear.

Numbness overtook me. Tasks became rote affairs. Objects lost their use-value. My intuition left me and I could no longer judge others' characters with accuracy. Though I felt like I finally understood these dull creatures, my understanding brought no satisfaction. Abstractions became vague. Tripping in the street one day, my eyes landed an inch from a pavement crack. It widened into a canyon. I stood up and shoegazed across a sewer grate. The void gaped. An odorless void, empty of the usual delirious fumes from below. Even a headache was beyond me. Migraines are at least proof of life. I felt nothing. I lost the scent of God. Nothing white, only black. There was no rot or decay in *this* black. Only absence.

Thus I entered my period of olfactory nihilism. I expected nothing from the future. Desired nothing. I did not feel like 'I.' My memory began to fade. No madeleine or steaming cup of tea could make the past relatable. I lay in bed for some months.

As a mouth-breather in a metropolis, I began to develop some minor lung issues. A wheeze, a cough here and there at first. The condition was exacerbated by my open window. I awoke one morning in a hacking fit. The metal fastening of my clothespin had come loose. The tape around my nasal bridge had lost most of its adhesiveness. My right nostril inhaled a sweet combination. A scent of fullness and freedom. Fresh budding plants. I tore the hanging contraption from my nose and followed the scent. Downstairs. Out the back. Around the side to the street.

There through the store window, I gazed at the bulbs on display. The halo of a rose bouquet danced and flickered with the shuffle of flaming hair behind it. Through the cracks in the door her perfume hit me with sensuous notes of deep, rich florals. I stood for a long moment inhaling. The ring of the scentless silver bell above the door filled my head with nuptial longings as my confident nose bobbed above the aisles.

"Hi." She smiled, beaming glimpses of purity. I opened my mouth to answer. The nose had different ideas. A deep breath filled my lungs with mint toothpaste. "What can I help you with?"

"I need some flowers."

"You came to the right place. What's the occasion?"

I met her herbal gaze, flinching at the punch of her vinegary eyeliner.

"I think your makeup has expired."

"Excuse me?"

"Romance."

"What?"

"The occasion. New girlfriend, prospective wife."

"Oh. Things are moving fast huh?"

"They will be once she gets the flowers."

"Hmm, okay..." She wrinkled her Roman nose. Soft, thin, anatomically flawless. I knew she was the woman for me. "A rose bouquet always sends the right message."

(Deep breath.) "Rose, yes. And violet, orchid, jasmine, orange blossom. Lily of the Valley."

"Wow, specific. Well let me just see what I can—"

"—Ylang-ylang too."

"Sorry, we don't carry that species."

"Sandalwood, oakmoss."

"Those aren't flowers."

"They're base notes."

"What?"

"*Red Door*, by Elizabeth Arden."

She stared. I continued.

"It's lovely. I could smell it from outside, even over the flowers." She took a slow step back from the counter. I hadn't showered in a while. "Would you go out to dinner with me?"

"No. I'm going to have to ask you to leave."

I thought of what to say. Something supportive, witty. The nose, again, intervened. I sneezed. Months of cloistered build-up erupted into my shielding hands. She placed a Kleenex on the edge of the counter.

"Thanks." Wiping alternated with coughing.

"Do you need some help? Like, a doctor?"

"Probably. Can I have another?"

"Are you going to buy any flowers?"

"They're a little out of my price range, actually."

She tore a second Kleenex from its box with two rosy fingernails and passed it to me.

Small acts of generosity are a good start to a relationship. I left the flower shop exhilarated. Night receded from my radius. In its place was a new color. Not red, strangely. Perhaps it was the hint of violet in her perfume. After that everything began to smell purple. I walked the streets feeling like a Roman emperor, robed in delight and privilege. Who knew that flowers, the most cliché and over-poeticized of phenomenon, could stir such sensations of emotional wealth and power?

The flower is not like the heart. Much has been made about the heart's beating, thumping, metaphorical centrality. But its connection with love is the most universal of category mistakes. I cannot dissociate that organ from the sour taste preceding cardiovascular blockage. The flower, however, is everything they say it is, the one metaphor that is accurately symbolized. Every other object of comparison is, like the heart, a category mistake—though not in the way that earlier empiricists thought. I crystallized this insight into an axiom:

1. *Every figurative comparison between two objects is really a comparison between the hidden smells which the qualities of those objects govern.* More rarely, a metaphor may be between two abstract processes rather than concrete objects, as such, in which case smell also plays a vital, though once-removed, role. It is these smells that form the fundamental relationship

between two things or processes being compared. Poets, the most malicious offenders of this category mistake, are notoriously obtuse on this point. With their unrepentant emphasis on language, they refuse to acknowledge the literal significations underlying their figurative speech.

The section of my treatise subtitled "Olfactory Poetics" intends to correct this long-standing error, as well as to introduce my theory about the Reanimation of the Author. It will go something like this: though a centuries-old writer may be both 1) dead, and 2) mysterious, their pages always give off a distinct smell of authorship. The *Beowulf* Poet betrayed himself in the dragon's breath around the burnt edges of his parchment. He was clearly a Saxon who, living in a cold climate, liked to stay warm around the hearth dreaming up monsters. From this we can surmise that he was employed in a Northumbrian court. Since the manuscript's staleness reeks of the early 8th century, he was almost certainly the royal fire-stoker to King Aldfrith.

Or take the case of Shakespeare: was he really Francis Bacon, or the Earl of Oxford, or de Vere? The truth is, could any of these alternate selves aptly handle the stench of his dramatic imagery? The Swan of Avon well knew the impossibility of the rose's mistaken identity, the scandal of cinnamon, the ascription of fickleness to violets when one is spurned, the reluctant lesser evil of choosing to live with cheese and garlic in a windmill over the company of a barbarous magician. So who was Shakespeare, then? As with roses, a bard with any other name would smell as sweet; the name is not important. If we must attach an appellation to him, however, Bacon seems the most likely nominee. It is a name that envelops all around it with the overpowering attribution of pig grease. His essay "Of Gardens" shows a remarkable nose for detail when he says, "That which above all others yields the sweetest smell is the violet." Sweetness, as we know, is not incompatible with falseness and fraud. Bacon discovered this when, at the height of his career, he was thrown in the Tower. He had more than enough time to toss off some plays there.

With my newfound zest for life, I resumed working on my treatise on olfactory empiricism with fervor, writing on scraps of this and that in the intervals between migraines and sudden naps—the usual chocolate wrappers (fun size, standard, king size), but also envelopes, napkins, cheesecloth. I keep them in various drawers and await an organizing editor. A purple nose takes a surprising toll on purple prose. My napping became more frequent. During naps I am not myself, I have no memory. And yet...while I sleep, I smell. Smelling guides dreaming. While awake, migraines disturb my conscious life and processing. Remembrance is increasingly impossible without a whiff of household chemical bottles to jolt me back to the present. These reflections led to my next axiom:

1. *Aromatic continuity is the source of self-identity.* What am I? An agglomeration of smells. Who am I? The name acting as a convenient shorthand for those agglomerations. What did I do yesterday? Peeled an orange. Wrote a thought on the back of the peel concerning the nature of 'orangeness.' Threw the orange out the window. What endures between 'orangeness' and the 'appleness' I uncovered the day before? Me—a being with a schnoz. The schnoz is the record of permanence.

My romantic life, being a subdivision of the nasal life, started looking up. The woman from the flower shop eventually agreed to go out with me. (I will not bore you with the details of my persistence or the number of bouquets I gave her after she sold them to me.) For our first date I took her to a French restaurant.

"This is a nice place," she said.

"Yeah, it's one of my favorites."

"I didn't peg you for a guy who would ever eat at a place like this."

"Fine dining is pretty affordable if you do it right."

Our waiter, an irritable chap who had served me before, maintained his composure upon seeing I was not alone and listed the specials. With his long black hair and mustache he somewhat resembled Descartes. I respected the clear and distinct way he enunciated his unpronounceables. He seemed, however, to possess an innate idea of his cultural superiority. It was my mission as a recurring patron to demonstrate that his refinement was merely acquired. I studied Violet as she looked over the menu. She seemed to be reading it, but I couldn't be sure (I'm good at pretending too). After she ordered I pointed to something. Surprise is vital to the nasal life.

"I'm impressed you can speak French," I said to Violet.

"Don't you? You said this was your favorite restaurant."

"I avoid the Rationalist tradition."

"That's an odd thing to say."

"For an empiricist, nothing particular is odd."

"A what?"

"An empiricist. A person who acquires knowledge through the senses, as defined by John Locke."

"*John Locke*...I think I've heard of him. He was an inventor or something, right?"

I felt a migraine coming on and gripped my head.

"Are you okay?" asked Violet.

Dinner arrived. I perked up.

"Yes, perfect."

Violet unrolled her silverware and placed her napkin on her lap. "It smells delicious," she said, rolling up the pasta with her fork. I concurred, hovering over my steamy plate, absorbing the nuances. She arched an eyebrow.

"What are you doing?"

"Enjoying my meal."

"Aren't you going to take a bite?"

"Why would I want to ruin my appetite?"

"You look hungry. You could stand to put on a few pounds."

"That's not really my style." I breathed in a blend of olive oil, thyme, and rosemary. Hints of the Holy Land. "Say, there's something I'm curious about if you don't mind me asking." She looked hesitant but said nothing. "You wouldn't happen to know—and it's totally fine if you don't want to share personal details—but um, I was wondering...what's your olfactory recognition score?"

"Why did I expect you would say something random like that?"

"Seems like a pretty obvious question to me."

"Do you know your olfaca...whadidyacallit?"

"Olfactory recognition score. Of course I know mine, who wouldn't?"

"And?"

"It's off the charts. The highest in existence."

She swirled her wine glass and laughed. "I think I'm starting to get it now."

I laughed with her. It was a peculiar feeling. Comedy is, in many ways, a betrayal of nasal authenticity. A carnival for the mouth. The nose was created to be a thing higher, set apart. The most dignified and stoical of orifices. It must remain ever aloof from oral behaviors. To cleanse my attitude, I took another gourmet whiff. My stomach growled. It wasn't supposed to do that. It had been trained to resist. The room blurred. I began to swoon.

"Are you okay?" She asked.

"Fine. Why?"

"You look pale. I mean—you're always pale, but you look even more pale than usual."

"You're right. I'm full. Probably...go. Before. Check."

That was the last thing I remember before my face fell into my plate.

I awoke in a sanitized room. I would not call it a *white* room, exactly, as that is a term I reserve for the olfactory purity of the metaphysical realm. But to others, it would have resembled a white room. My eyes adjusted to the strawberry-haired woman sitting next to me.

"Violet?"

"My name is Meagan."

"Oh, I'm sorry...I didn't know."

"We met three months ago."

"But you smell purple."

"Haven't heard that one. Um, it didn't seem right to leave you after you passed out at the restaurant. I wanted to make sure you're okay."

I reached out for her hand.

"Will you marry me?"

"No. You're weird," she said as she pulled away.

"Figures. *It shall be fickle*, said the Bard of the violet."

"He wrote that about Adonis."

"Point is, in this case you're the violet."

"I'm a Meagan."

"My Venus!"

"You're too much. Really. I'm glad you're okay, though. I've got to be going."

Violet stood up to leave but stopped as the doctor entered.

"You're a lucky man," he told me.

"Thanks." *Did he have access to my charts?* "It's nice to be validated." *Had he seen my huge ORS?*

The doctor's face took on a serious expression. "You almost didn't make it, Mr. Keene. Do you know why you lost consciousness?"

I elucidated the consequences of my divine capacity. The doctor looked at Violet, who shrugged her shoulders. "He just comes in my store a lot."

The doctor continued: "How long have you been experiencing fatigue, nausea, headaches, dizziness?"

"Depends on how you define those things."

"Let's go with the standard dictionary definitions."``

"In that case, hard to say exactly." I followed the gaps in aromatic identity. "Years."

"Ok...what about loss of appetite? Weight loss?"

I explained that corporeal shrinking was common among those who commune with hyperreality. The doctor nodded.

"What are you getting at, doc?" I asked.

"You have Addison's Disease."

The divine capacity, a disease? I'd heard the lies before.

"Your adrenal gland doesn't produce enough cortisol. The low blood pressure it causes is a life-threatening condition, Mr. Keene. It can kill you."

"What can you do?" asked Violet.

"We already did it," said the doctor. He turned back to me. "We treated your adrenal insufficiency with a corticosteroid injection."

I shook his hand. "Thank you doctor. You've saved me, I'm grateful. Now I can continue with my important work."

"Oh, where do you work?"

"My apartment. Technically, well...I'm unemployed. What I meant was, my intellectual labors. When my treatise is published it's going to overturn the foundations of what we think we know about empiricism."

"That's nice. When will it be published?"

"After someone organizes my candy wrappers."

The doctor looked at Violet, who shrugged her shoulders. He continued: "You'll be free to go soon. We'd just like to monitor you for the night."

A nurse brought in a plastic dinner tray. "Hungry?" She planted it on my lap. I leaned into the rising steam and inhaled. I felt the heat, but only faint scents. Cheap hospital food had no nuance. Sensing my reluctance, the nurse spoon-fed me. The vegetables were mushy and bland. The barbeque sauce on the meatloaf was barely sweet.

"This food tastes expired," I said.

"Oh, that reminds me," the doctor said, whirling at the door, "—we fixed your nose."

I gulped the meatloaf down without chewing. "What do you mean you *fixed it*? My nose did not need fixing."

"I mean you can smell like everybody else now. Your hypersensitivity was one of the side effects of cortisol deficiency."

I stared at the wall, struggling to process the words. *Like everybody else.*

"You'll need to take a hormone supplement, but there's no reason you can't live a normal life from here on out."

A normal life. My olfactory axioms crumbled before me.

The doctor looked at Violet. "Is he okay?"

"He'll be fine," she said. "It just needs to sink in. I think he thought it was a genetic thing."

The cascading odoratura of Violet is faded from me now. In her place, a bright but flavorless Meagan brings flowers from her shop that go unsold at the end of each day. A kaleidoscope of petals with wilting edges surrounds my bed. I stuff my nose in their stamens and draw their stems along the underside of my nostrils. Pale, passionless pleasures. Each bouquet is like a rainbow that, losing its sparking mists, gradually disappears from the sky.

I have yet to work up the courage to ask Meagan about her olfactory recognition score again after she avoided the question at dinner that night. Whatever it is, it must be higher than mine now. I try not to seem envious, but she sometimes catches me ogling her perfect nose.

Sitting at my desk, I go through my assortment of old philosophical scraps. Insights of a man possessed. Of a demigod cast down from the omnifragrant heights. My knowledge of God has devolved into the ordinary faith-based variety. Since my hospital visit, I am reconciling to a world where whiteness is synonymous with cleanliness. Sterility has neutralized the sugar.

As my imagination sputters out a few mundane thoughts, Meagan comes into the room and puts a bottle in my hand. "Don't forget."

"I won't." I smile as she leaves. When she is gone, I stare at the bottle. *Take one pill twice a day,* the label reads. I begin to unscrew the cap, then pause. I open a desk drawer and toss the bottle in. Slipping a Hershey's bar from my pocket, I remove the chocolate from its gold foil, flatten the wrapper in front of me with its thick paper backing facing up, and place the bar on a stack of books to the left of my head, near my nose. I uncap a black permanent marker, sniff the ink tip, and write an axiom:

1. *It may be possible to know things without first smelling them.* Whether such things are worth knowing is an ethical question. A treatise on nasal values would be necessary to answer it.

Nose Candy

Humphrey Primp & Johanna A. Fromond

Any second (*anag.*)
      Candy knows any second...
Candy knows any second something...
Candy knows any second something dramatic...
Candy knows any second something dramatic might...
Candy knows any second something dramatic might happen...

Italo Calvino and Faye Dunaway never got into a canoe together and gently paddled along the Speed River. It never happened. It could never have happened. At any time. It would be an anachronism. A fiction. But, of course, so many things that could never have happened are so very much like things that do and things that have happened. Many things that likely happened, but did not, are also so similar to things that are unbelievable but *did* happen, that the weave and weft of perceived realisms is richly textured and shifting.

Eugène Ionesco and H.P. Lovecraft never ever had tea, of any kind, or a bottle of 1932 Barolo together. It would be darned absurd to suggest so. You would be stitching people up if you said so. *Absurditas* (against deafness) / *Absurdus* (untuned/discordant).

Think of any unlikely combination - Captain Kidd and Peter Pan - Joris-Karl Huysmans and Marcus Aurelius, etc., *et cetera*. Captain Hook and Tinkerbell...

But, yes, so very many things that could never ever happen are also almost exactly like the things that do happen. Fact is stranger than fiction, it is said. And, often, the only real way to unpack and understand fact is to consider its fiction. The mirror image.

Charlie Chaplin did not shake hands with Leonard Cohen. And, to be clear, Leonard Cohen never shook hands with Charlie Chaplin, on or off screen.

When Italo Calvino did not get into a canoe with Faye Dunaway on the Speed River, and when Ionesco and H.P. Lovecraft never shared Earl Grey nor vino, something in the fabric of the world changed. The handshake between Chaplin and Cohen that never happened, altered reality.

Possibilities were negated when these things did not happen. Alternate kinetic versions were avoided. But, they do however remain as potentials - like dust on eyelashes - like the sub-vocalizations you "sound" when you read to yourself (that voice in your head - the one that can recall and sing songs, without you ever making a sound). You know.

Candy knows that any second the certainties, like a summer soirée of mythic customaries, waver into reflections of an anagram of any second. Into pseudo-surrealism. As quasisensical. Inside Para'Pataphysics.

The solutions of imaginary science

Candy knows any second something mundane may happen...

The canoe Italo and Faye did not go a-paddling in was so very very beautiful, and Humphrey was wrong, it was the Eramosa River that skirts the south side of Guelph - not the Speed River that flows into the Eramosa, for Italo and Faye were definitely not on The Speed, neither on the Eramosa for that matter.

Poor Calvino and Dunaway did not experience this very very beautiful birch bark canoe. It was light as a feather, the sleek paddles created whirls upon whirls on the surface of the Eramosa. Ah, the things that do not happen!

Candy asked "why?"

The Eramosa River was never visited by Samuel Beckett and Gertrude Stein, in a raft - Nag and Nell as paddlers. That never happened. Samuel and Gertrude would have loved it.

Candy tried to sleep. (...interesting to note that Sumac is backwards for Camus)

Candice was gripping tight to the rails of the ship - the turbulent sea charging the vessel at dramatic rhythmic angles and impossible slopes - salty sea spray thrown against her face. The old three-masted clipper was at the end of her days. Candice held on. The sound of old wood creaking. An ancient shanty...

Candorra of the High Seas

> *Oh*! *Hey*! *Ho*!
> The ship rocked
> The ship rocked for Heaven
> and Hell
> and Haven
> and Hole,
> and the other place too
> And the other place, the other place
> *Aaand* the other place too
> *Ho*! *Hey*! *Oh*!

Italo was on the wooden jetty - and he saw Faye. She blushed. Her hair swept into flowing waves by a scented breeze.

But, of course this did not happen.

But, that never happened either - she woke up.

Ah, the things that do not happen - so vital to the things that do. Some of the things that happen depend for their existence upon the things that do not happen. It is a fiction and a fact.

No, I will not mention counting. No numbers here.

A scene of Italo and Faye making their own canoe:

Such a thin skin against all that water - as the fish have. A wood meniscus

Like a puppet in Noh plays

"Back to the ship, Captain!" (The canoe)

And, on a sunny sandy beach there was a mobile tented theatre and marionettes - you know Punch - you know Judy - you know Pere Ubu - Pinocchio:

"The marionette stood motionless with staring eyes, open mouth, and the broken egg-shell still in his hands" (Collodi)

The theme of today's Puppet Opera is to make a crossword. The characters will call out clues and you have to think really hard and focus. It is a very very beautiful sunny day at the seaside.

Wall's ice-cream, beach balls, splashing. And the little audience in front of the colourfully striped tent theatre. All the children laughing and screaming "Look BEHIND You!!"

Williknocks:
"Across
1: Y and Cones (*anag.*)"

Mrs Halfpenny:
"Down
1: Sony Dance (*anag.*)"

All the children yell "Look BEHIND You!"

Williknocks and Mrs Halfpenny and Doodles the Dog (together):
"Diagonally
1.5: Andy Scone (*anag.*)"

All the children scream and holler and jump up and down waving their arms like crazy

Mrs Halfpenny (*aside*):
"Upside Down
2.75: Any Second (*anag.*)"

Candy knows any second
Something...
Something unusual...

Something unusual is...
Something unusual is unfolding...

The very very beautiful feather-light canoe lazed down Eramosa River unmoored, empty. The sea shanty out in the ocean storm wafted away in the sea spray. The ship disappeared - it did not sink, it simply stopped being. The sunny seaside beach is very very empty. There is no colourful tented theatre, no children. Only the screech of myriad gulls and the rolling waves can be seen and heard - the lunar heartbeat. A lonely tanker is out there on the clear horizon and a ferry is plying its way across the waves. Perhaps there are many people on the ferry.

Italo Calvino and Faye Dunaway and Eugène Ionesco and H.P. Lovecraft and Captain Kidd and Peter Pan and Captain Hook and Tinkerbell and Joris-Karl Huysmans and Marcus Aurelius and Charlie Chaplin and Leonard Cohen and Samuel Beckett and Gertrude Stein and Nag and Nell and Camus and *Candorra of the High Seas* and Punch and Judy and Pere Ubu and Pinocchio and Collodi and Williknocks and Mrs Halfpenny and Doodles the Dog and Andy Scone and Candy and Humphrey Primp all exist(ed), some between what actually happened and what was meant to happen and what was not meant to happen and what never ever happened at all.

The illusions of imaginary science...

Candy knows any second is an anagram, that Y and Cones too, and Sony Dance, and even Andy Scone are all, every single one of them, nose candy...

The canoe had eyes. Very very beautiful eyes. You see. Eyes painted on its prow. To see its way.

If it blink it sink!

So they are eternally open, staring out ahead over the waves. Look Behind You!

It is an adventurous voyage, how Ionesco did not see Sinbad in his ship. Sinbad navigating treacherous currents and cliffy shores, but never seeing Ionesco. Faye said something. Sinbad did not, ever, hear her. Italo had a dream, perhaps - not of Sinbad (or maybe he did), but of Faye saying something, in a film, surely an anachronism.

The eyes looked ahead.

All aboard asleep. Including the cat, Sweet Jupiter.

The canoe did not sleep - did not close its eyes - could not blink, or it would visit the riverbed and sleep forever.

A canoe can go both ways - Italo invited Faye onto a canoe with eyes painted at both ends, bow and stern - in whatever direction of rowing - so it could see afore and aft. Before and After. "Look Behind You" was now redundant. Look from left to right instead: sinister and dexter.

Candy knows, any second is an anagram of "nose candy". And that is meaningful - perhaps it never really happened. Perhaps it did. Or will.

Beckett and Candice lay dozing in a canoe with ears painted on its hull.

The things that happen negate the myriad of things that don't happen. But, not quite. No. You know. Candy knows, any second a canoe might blink.

And all of the multitude of things that never happen keep on never happening, again and again. For ever more. You see.

Candy knows, any second...

It keeps on not happening.

Postscript ***1

Humphrey is on the beach watching his idea float out there on the tide. Italo Calvino whispers in his ear - something about a disappearing knight, ye knowest.

Faye Dunaway winks at him (Italo, and maybe also Mr Primp).

Beckett dozes off, again

Lovecraft grumbles.

Chaplin silently waddles off with his bamboo cane.

Jarry cycles through another town.

Humphrey watches Candy, Candice watches Humphrey...

They are in a very very beautiful canoe, on the Speed River - named by John Galt, the nineteenth century Scottish writer, founder of Guelph one month after Beethoven's funeral.

Humphrey says:

"Any Second..."

Johanna says, like a vintage seaside postcard:

"Looking forward to seeing you and hearing all about it"

Postscript ***2

Candy put her pen down and looked over at Humphrey - there lazing in the bow of the very very beautiful canoe. Such a very very beautiful sunny day. Birds bathing. Memory of a beach theatre - Look Behind You - ice-cream - Faye smiling. None of it ever happened.

The things that did happen were imbued with a deep timeless beauty because of those things that never happened.

You know. He knows Candy. Any second...

Appendix A

Examples of things that did happen:

Bertolt Brecht slammed his glass down on the worn wooden table.

Francis Bacon fell over.

Beckett dozed.

Italo nodded and smiled.

Faye waved goodbye.

Nose Candy
Michael Lauria

"**M**arwi's Wonder-works," reads the weathered bronze sign, with letters accentuated by golden paint, cracked and flaking from time and weathering. It is attached to the side of a lone, multi-story stone building. The structure is illuminated by small globules of light, glowing and hovering randomly around. The Wonder-works stands alone in the crowded city of Anank, surrounded by empty lots. The lots are filled with rubble and twisted metal, maybe a sign of neglect, or perhaps of a misfortune of the past. The empty space around the property in this dense city almost gives the impression that the other buildings are shying away or keeping their distance.

The evening mists that are always expected in the city arrive on schedule, just after the day's final light has retreated behind the mountains far away. The mist this night brings a wanderer to the Wonderworks. The figure is wrapped in a dark cloak, with the billowing hood pulled up to assist the shadows that are obscuring their form. A mask, deep red and made of a soft cloth, is pulled up over the figure's lower face, leaving only their eyes uncovered. Such concealment in this city wouldn't seem out of place, masks and cloaks are seen as a fashion choice as well as a mark of station with many of the locals. The figure's eyes, however, are not so ordinary. Both are large and many would say quite memorable. The right eye is a soft green that is slightly luminescent in the night, the left a striking amber color, also carrying a soft glow. Underneath the left eye on the skin is a set of small tattoos or markings that resemble clockwork gears interlocking, and some strange script of curving and twisting symbols. A delicate looking hand wrapped in strips of tight black cloth reaches out from the shadows of the cloak toward a thick hanging chain by the front entrance of the stone building. There is a slight hesitation as a breath is taken in, the figure steeling itself before taking the next step, pulling the chain.

Metal on metal grinding and squealing can be heard as the wanderer pulls forcefully on the chain that awakens a clockwork mechanism inside the building. A deep bell tolls within, as the multiple locks slowly release their hold and the door loosens and creaks open. The visitor pushes past the heavy door just enough to slide their lithe form through into the rooms beyond. Their eyes dart around seeing the warmly lit antechamber and the lack of any real decoration or furnishings. A trail of lanterns ignite slowly, illuminating the proper path a guest should follow. This guest however knows different, and walks to a hall opposite the lantern trail. Sliding a bit of dark wood paneling, they reveal a hidden hall and silently move in and close the panel behind. Their eyes glow softly as they make their way down the long hall, turning at the end and heading down a set of stone stairs.

Coming to the bottom of the stairs, the figure stops at a door and knocks, just once, then waits. They stand in absolute silence for quite some time, knowing that to knock again would be against the protocols that they had learned long before. Finally, the door opens to a large room, smokey and dim with glows of various colors and large ominous shadows creeping about the walls. The visitor steps in and their eyes dart around, seeing that everything is virtually the same as every other time. Shelves upon shelves of objects, a vast collection of them, some sparkling and valuable looking, some intricate and artistic, others broken or vile. There are jars of things, creatures of various types, some unknown to most, their eyes all staring at the visitor, all watching the movement. An acrid scent wafts by as they walk past a sputtering, smoking brass object. Swirling plumes of smoke dance through the air, hinting at charred resins, tar and harsh chemicals. Their eyes starting to water, they quicken their pace, enough to pass a few other trinkets issuing similar pungent vapors. The visitor's eyes show a bit of annoyance with the odors and effects of this part of the collection.

"You can drop the shadow and anonymity. We've been through this before, and you're doing work for me. It's a waste of your effort and my time." The gravelly stern voice comes from behind a few shelves, as the small hunched form of the ancient owner of The Wonder-works, Marwi, makes his presence known. He shuffles past a few of the larger devices in the collection. The thin, ruddy-faced individual has wisps of white hair atop his speckled head, and tiny sharp eyes that resemble burning coals with their color and intensity. His large twisted ears sport shocks of unruly hair extending in all directions.

The visitor shrugs and visibly sighs, as they lower the hood and release control of the shadows that wrapped their body and cloak. The shadows shrink away, returning to their proper place on the feminine form of the visitor as she is revealed. Though she is still masked, the cloak no longer hides her dancer-like frame as it had before. The uncovered portions of her head and face are now illuminated by the dim light of the room. Wild snow white hair is corralled back into an equally wild, short ponytail tipped in a dark red color matching the deep red of her mask. Whirling tousled bangs, also tipped in red, frame her face as an annoyed expression can be plainly read in her eyes. "I'm more comfortable with the security of shadows." Her soft voice carries a slight raspy quality and a unique, unplaceable accent.

Marwi smirks at her reaction and waves his unusually spindly fingers at her comment as if waving it away from existence. "I have no care for your comfort, you opted for this form of payment. Remember you still owe me."

The woman calmly interjects, "Not for much longer. After this, my debt is paid, and you give me the final piece."

Marwi tilts his head, "Correct, that is, until you need another impossible solution."

The wanderer nods with a slight scowl, "We'll see. What is it this time, a monster's secret prize, a collector's illegal procurement, a noble's lost heirloom?" She looks amused, listing off various tasks in the line of her past jobs for the "miracle worker".

"Sweets!" the twisted old being shoots back.

The response causes a look of disbelief and concern, as she knows it to be too simple a request. "No, really, what are ya after?" She tilts her head waiting for the explanation that was sure to come.

"Sweets! The delicious, mouth-watering memories of perfect confections and the delight they bring," the ancient one reveals, with a sound of menacing glee and delight at the look of alarm taking to the eyes of his help.

"Wait, part of the deal: no children... no innocents..." the visitor starts to protest before she is cut off by Marwi again.

"No, no children... and definitely not innocent. This is a debt being called for account." He tinkers with a few baubles beside him as he explains, "A very old debt never repaid. My previous attempts to collect have been met with apprehension and denial."

Her curiosity piqued, she chances to discover more. "So, why this, why now, why-"

His gaunt features twist into something she had never seen on his face before, a smile. It is a sight that could haunt the sleepless nights of those that behold it.

"Why you? It's delightful dear, you who have lost so much of yourself, wresting a valuable memory from the grasp of the one who denies me my payment for our bargain. It makes it that much sweeter a conclusion."

His eyes burn bright as he continues "What will I do with it? Well, should you prove again successful, then, well, perhaps I will reveal that deliciousness as a bonus to your own debt being paid."

She shifts uncomfortably and nods, internalizing his words a bit, dwelling on her own dealings with the Wonder-works of Marwi. She inhales and nods, "Then tell me how ya want me to gather the memories. Not from a corpse right?"

Marwi's expression looks almost as if he were wounded by her inquiry. "Corpse, Corpse," he sputtered. "My dear, I make miracles and wonder. I'm not a butcher or a grave robber. Besides, that's ignorant." His voice is coated in derision, "Living memories that vivid, from a corpse, don't be ridiculous, lass, and here I thought you as bright." He gathers himself quietly as he looks at her eyes and sees he has made his point clear and shamed her sufficiently.

His spidery hands dive into various pockets hidden in his dark clothing, searching for the answer to her question. He produces a modest-sized green velvet bag and holds it out to her.

These will help you in that matter, and I leave the finding of him and the procurement up to you." He looks at her with a scowl, his wiry, twisting, smokey white eyebrows that defy physics accentuating the look. "Any more help and it's not worth what you owe me."

Pulling up her hood and gathering her cloak around herself, she grabs the bag of tools her employer holds out for her. "Do I at least get a name, then?"

The Miracle Worker starts shuffling back into the shelves of his collections, already busying himself with whatever tasks he had previously been engaged in. A whirr of a gadget of some sort, a squeak of a small animal, and a raspy laugh can be heard, followed by a few small crashes of objects falling to the stone floor. The visitor sighs and grumbles to herself, looking impatient, before Marwi calls out distantly but oddly clear, "Ambrose Pasoka."

"That Ambrose Pasoka, the ancient genius who created delights and treats that are said to sway the mind and emotions with but a taste." She breathes in the night air deeply, taking in the familiar scents, as she walks along the streets of the misty city wrapped again in her shadows.

Continuing to whisper to herself. "Finding was never an issue, I have a name. I can always find 'em." She looks up at the large buildings of the vast city of Anank, looking at each stone building adorned with large metal clockwork, pipes, and assorted chimneys billowing plumes of various colored smoke.

"Even in the city of Destiny, I can find 'em." She huffs a bit in annoyance, "But he is known, has sway and a following in a town where one can get anything. Won't be easy getting to 'em."

She stops as she spies the glimmers of dawn starting to crest the horizon of the buildings before her. How long had she been wandering this evening, she wondered to herself. A clicking of her tiny metallic clockwork tattoos is heard. The marks, which had been shifting and moving like grinding gears, slow and stop. The shadows that conceal her retreat to their proper place, and her amber eye flickers as she moves her attention to a large building adorned with the tell-tale signs of a tavern or club of some sort. A few stumbling patrons head home before the light of day totally fills the sky, one of which is singing a merry tune. The owner or operator walks another out to meet an entourage of caretakers.

The large hairy creature dressed in a fine suit, almost carrying the well-dressed yet sloppy-looking patron who apparently was having trouble standing on his own, proclaims in a gruff yet refined voice, "He's all yours ladies, make sure he gets home and gets some rest."

One of the waiting staff gives a nod as she carefully supports the obviously drunken elderly patron.

"Will do Barlo, he'll be back tonight for sure." She winks to the large proprietor as she passes the drunk to her companion, who hoists him up in large strong arms and begins to carry him off.

"Come on mister Pasoka, let's get some rest so you can celebrate some more," she remarks as they begin making their way down the road to an elaborate carriage.

"Always find 'em," she remarks aloud, realizing she had garnered the attention of the owner of the establishment.

"What business have you, lass?"

She tilts her head at the large tavernkeep. Her eyes smile before she speaks up with little hesitation. "Hopin' there is time for a mug before ya close."

In response the large bestial head shakes, "Sorry Lass. Closed up for a bit, come back this evening for a drink an' a treat."

"A Treat?" she asks, "Sounds interestin.'"

A nod of confidence and a large snaggly toothed grin meet her query. "Yes lass, we are hosting an event with the famed Confectioner, Ambrose-"

She finishes the name with him, "Pasoka."

He nods and continues, "Quite. We are in the middle of a multi-day contest. Pasoka has wagered a fortune that he can create a new confection to match any meal and any spirit that our local up-and-comers create, every night for a whole moon cycle."

"He's been victorious then?" she asks, quite curious about this news, to which the business owner raises a finger,

"Almost. Still has a few more eves, but every night the party gets bigger and bigger."

She nods, "Can anyone challenge 'em? I'm living in the city and have traveled quite a bit and picked up some amazingly delicious and diverse recipes and spirits."

The owner gives a hearty laugh, "Sorry, invite only. But you can enjoy the festivities and try some amazing bites and spirits. Maybe meet the contestants." He pauses and looks deeply into her eyes a moment before continuing his thought. "Tell you what, 'cause I like your eyes and manner, you get here at sundown and I'll have saved a good seat for you."

She gives a slight giggle in response, "Sure, ya sure I can't get a little sip before then?" She holds up her fingers pinching the air, emphasizing how little she was asking for.

The large owner yawns and shakes his head in rejection, "At sundown. I need my sleep too."

The wanderer nods, accepting defeat, and gives a wave, "Save me a nice seat, g'morning." The large tavern owner waves his large hand and lumbers back into the building, shutting the door behind him.

"So, that's the in, is it? Should be easy enough," she speaks quietly to herself, alone in the morning mist. "Minimal hunting, I know where he'll be, have an in to meet 'em. Just got to wait, watch, and not drink too much."

Her brow furrows as she stands there thinking it over. "So, this requires me to take a memory, an important one no doubt, from this confectionary legend."

She sighs with the conflict that has crept into her planning. "Ugh, I'm someone who has constantly sought to reclaim my own memories and protect what I still have, and I'm to steal away one of his." She pauses as she notes the shadows hiding from the sun. Gears and all manner of machinery that are part of the buildings seem to spring to life as the sleeping city wakes.

"Okay, why? Why am I willing to do this?" she asks herself in a whisper before quickly answering herself, "Because you will be out from under Marwi's thumb. You will have repaid him for the mask and you will finally get that key. More valuable than even he knows. A debt repaid and one of my belongings returned."

She nods, "A debt is owed to Marwi and Pasoka hasn't paid. The laws of this city are on my side this time. It's what makes Anank work. The city where one can find whatever they imagine and seek, for a price."

Her quiet contemplation is interrupted by the sudden noise of an oncoming coach barrelling towards her and the curses of its driver. She nimbly slides from its path, in a blur, with little effort. The driver winces, not seeing the movement and expecting a collision, and looks flabbergasted from the lack of impact and the missing sound of a body being sundered as the clockwork vehicle continues along its path.

A scowl crosses her face as she shakes her head, "Time for some rest. Then you shall enjoy the festivities." She dashes into the thin alley nearby and disappears into the city's growing movement as it wakes.

The daytime in Anank is a blur of motion and commerce, its inhabitants seeking fortune, making deals and living life, as the wanderer hopes to dream in her day's rest.

The long shadows of night eventually find their way into the city, accompanied by the mist, as all but a few of the mechanics of the various buildings slowly halt for the evening. The nightlife in this particular neighborhood is generally small and relegated to a few restaurants, clubs, and taverns. One place, though, stands out as being busier and more lively than the rest. Barlo's Battleground, or as some like to add flourish, The Battleground of Culinary Glory. While it was first known as a place for a good drink and a respectable meal, it has, over the years, gained more of a reputation for its events. Gastronomic challenges are made, and the tavern serves as the backdrop for amazing culinary grudges settled. This event is only a little different as it is an invitation to challenge the creativity of one of the most renowned confectioners known in the lands, Ambrose Pasoka.

The wanderer has made her way inside as early as possible to take in the layout and get a feel for the venue. As promised, Barlo has saved her a choice table near one reserved for the VIPs. She thumbs the small velvet bag absent-mindedly as she takes in the unique decor of the tavern. The Battleground name isn't so much something to do with culinary challenges as it seems to be the choice in decor. Old weaponry and bits of armor are hanging from the walls, while a few display cases have better preserved and cared for weapons in them. The walls also have hanging various poorly done landscapes labeled with the location and the famous victory or defeat that took place. One particular wall that all the tables seem to almost be surrounding is covered in a large dark gold velvet curtain, like something out of a gaudy theater. Beside that is the bar where Barlo the large barkeep and owner finishes a drink and grabs a tray of a few more.

The wanderer smirks as Barlo delivers another full tankard to her. "So, the event?"

The large creature goes to respond but stops short as a commotion and cheers erupt from the doorway. "Ah. It's starting. Right about now."

In saunters two individuals. One is a shorter stocky person with a curvy figure, a short mop of dark azure hair with a few nub-like horns poking through, and short, trimmed beard on her chin. She is dressed in a clean, pale green and very utilitarian style of clothing, with a black apron in hand. She gives off an air of quiet confidence and contained energy as she casts a slight glare at the other individual. This is someone that the wanderer recognizes from the night before, but much more together and in control. A rotund masculine figure with a pale complexion and trimmed and curled mustache, his silvery hair is coated in a product to make it shiny and almost seem to be metal. His dress is nothing that a normal chef or confectioner would wear, and seems something more fitting for a noble attending a courtly event. To say his coat is ostentatious, with its lace, extra jeweled buttons, and gold trim, would be selling it short.

The rotund figure announces in a large blustery voice, "Tonight I, the King of Sweets Ambrose Pasoka, will face another challenger, and will create another original sugary masterpiece from my dreams, which all of you will get a taste."

He pauses as the room erupts with cheers. The wanderer looks to him with a curious smile, clapping along with the cheers around her as the cheering dies down.

"My challenger, a local whose family is a dynasty of chefs originally from the Frozen lands of Kion, Yongi Mellia." He again pauses for another round of cheering but it is slightly less ecstatic, giving the feeling that Yongi is clearly the underdog.

"Excuse me lass," Barlo leaves the tray at the table and wanders over to the wall with the gold curtain, tugging hard on some woven cords and revealing a large open kitchen that is split in two. The keen eyes of the wanderer pick up that bits of stone and brick of the original wall separating it from the rest of the tavern were still jutting from the floor and surrounding walls.

"At least it fits the battleground feel," she remarks to herself with a smile in her eyes.

The challenger speaks up, "Tonight you will face the perfection of a meal of pickled roast wooly lizard gizzards with root vegetables and Kion Ice Wine!"

A collective sound of shock and concern sweeps around the room at such an exotic sounding meal with a hard to come by protein. Then laughter is heard, deep bellowing laughter, "I don't fear your odd cuisine! I will make a treat full of joy and warmth to match and best your challenge!" proclaims Pasoka with an over the top wave of his arms and a flourish. The crowd again cheers as the two prepare to enter the kitchen.

Pasoka tilts his head toward the masked woman, "You." The wanderer points to herself, feeling a sudden flit of nervousness and concern over his attention to her presence. "Yes, with the eyes like gems. Watch my coat." He tosses his outrageously fancy coat to the suddenly dumbfounded woman, who quickly gathers herself for a response.

She restrains any bit of malice that had suddenly appeared in her heart and replies politely. "Of course, it will be an honor, and to return it to you over a drink when you are victorious."

He gives a wink to her and tweaks his mustache, "And you will taste my victory." He turns dramatically and saunters into his portion of the Kitchen.

"Let the cooking begin!" shouts Barlo over the din of the crowd, adding, "Also the bar will be in full swing while we watch and await our meals. There is as always a minimum cover for the meal and event."

The masked woman looks over the coat and finally sets it to the side and opens the small green bag and peeks in, half expecting to see something dangerous or complex. She withdraws a simple glass tube, filled with a clear liquid and labeled. It reads "Return to Marwi." Peering at it, she turns it up and down, trying to really look at it, and yet be casual and inconspicuous. Nodding to herself, she figures that this must be what she would be carrying the memory back in. She looks into the shadows of the bag for the other object that she had felt from the outside, a strange jewel. She blinks at it a bit. Why was Marwi so insistent on surprises.

"You're a bright girl, you'll figure it out." She had heard it too many times for it to really phase her as much as it had originally.

She pours the azure jewel out into her hand. It is cut and faceted intricately with golden inlay scripting in some strange writing she doesn't recognize. As she watches it, she revels in how beautiful it is and in the swirling brilliant blue hues. Then she notices the intense glittering. Suddenly she feels a pain in her amber eye, a searing heat. Quickly she slams her eyes shut and drops the jewel into the pouch. She growls silently to herself, recognizing the charm that almost had her and some memory that matched the parameters of the jewel. She was lucky she had her eye and her own charms to protect her. Shaking her head, she looks quickly around the busy room to see if anyone has noticed, and satisfied that the light show she had experienced was in her own mind, she fastens the bag closed and waves her hand for another drink.

The room is abuzz for the hours that pass, most are there to socialize and keep tabs on the tricks and culinary magic that is happening in the theater, cheering on their chosen side. A few are enjoying their own company and a strong drink, waiting for the meal. The wanderer has polished off a few tankards and decides it best to keep some sort of edge, expecting the inevitable occurrence: something unexpected.

Finally she notices Barlo making his way to the kitchens and beginning to talk with the waiting contestants. He then turns and announces, "Dinner and dessert is served!" The first few plates full of food are taken to a specific table, set the closest to the kitchens, where five individuals sit with dinnerware and a stack of parchment, inkwells, and pens.

"The judges will receive their food first, as is tradition, then a sampling will go to the other guests," Barlo dictates the actions before adding, "The reigning champion has made sure that all guests will have a full portion of his treat."

To which the room breaks out in applause which Pasoka seems to eat up, making exaggerated bows to his adoring fans. The event staff then scurry to portion, plate, and deliver small sampling plates to the crowd.

Receiving her plate, the wanderer looks at it closely. She is oddly familiar with some of the food of the North lands, and knows that if not pickled, any bit of the wooly lizards could be mildly toxic. She sees the telltale ombré of the meat's color that shows it had been treated correctly. She wonders a moment where that bit of knowledge came from, she isn't from that culture and has no memory of it otherwise. Perhaps one of her missing bits, she surmises, this sort of thing happens every so often, especially with the possibility of danger.

"At least this time I remembered before I dove in," she comments to herself with a slight amused look in her eyes.

Sliding the small bite under the mask to her mouth, she tastes the warm delicacy, savoring the tart juices from the brined meat before the truly deep flavors from the roasting overtake it, followed by the clean finish for the sauce. She eyes the root vegetables and subtly wraps them in a small bit of delicate green cloth and tucks them away. She waits a moment, sipping at the frigid ice wine, not wanting to taste too much because of its reputation for being extremely potent and cold.

The Wanderer pauses and looks at the odd and beautiful dessert course that Pasoka had produced. A truffle of sorts, from the initial look, with delicate beautiful ice-like crystals protruding from it like that of a cave formation. His reputation of being a whimsical dessert creator was definitely earned, if this was a common example of his work. She looks around the room, having noticed the usual din of the tavern is quite subdued and muffled. Everyone's mouth is full and their attention is solely on the food, including both contestants who have taken a seat at the table next to hers. She quickly notes that Pasoka's two employees, who had escorted him to his coach the night before, are quite close at hand. They are also enjoying the meal while watching the rest of the room. When one of the women's eyes are caught by the wanderer's attention, she quickly gives a wink and holds up the ice wine glass to Pasoka's employee. This garners a nod and a return of the gesture. Better to play up the interest than be more suspicious by quickly looking away, or at least she figures it has been the best course in the recent past.

Taking a knife she cuts into the confection, revealing a ruby center with a shimmering gel that slowly oozes out on the plate. Taking a small bite of the delicate dessert, she immediately feels some strange feeling. She starts to smile, the flavor is surprising, smooth and sweet, but also something else. It tugs at something somewhere, a happiness almost euphoric that teases at nostalgia before an emptiness overtakes her. It's interrupted by the familiar burning pain in her eye, another charm. She gasps quietly, thankful yet again to be wrenched free from the grip of whatever had teased at overtaking her. Her eyes dart around the room to look at all of the guests who had tried the dessert, lost in their own sweet dreams. A pang of jealousy grips her. As grateful as she is for her protections she is also aware that she felt something different than the others, the sense of loss that didn't show on a single face. Sighing, she tucks the remaining dessert away after wrapping it tightly in a large glossy leaf she has pulled from a pouch.

After most have finished with the meal, Barlo steps up to the curtain with a scroll in hand. The time has come to hear the result, and judging from the strange enchantment that the dessert held, it is hardly a surprise to the wanderer.

"Another astounding victory for Pasoka, how does he manage to make sweets so delightful?" bellows Barlo in joy and admiration.

"How indeed?" the Wanderer mutters to herself as the room explodes in cheers and celebration. A crowd pushes toward the table to congratulate the Master Confectioner, and of course politely pay respects to the creator of the exotic meal who lost. The masked woman waits and watches as Pasoka's help have their work cut out for them, keeping the festivities as orderly as needed to ensure security. Pasoka himself is devouring the attention, and singing his own praises as well. The loser, well into her third glass of ice wine, isn't holding any grudge it seems, as she celebrates with the victor. The intensity of the celebration is something that the Wanderer feels is familiar, but no memory can be attached to the sensation she is feeling, again this is nothing really new to her but she notes it. She thinks of Marwi and their deal, the mask, a trinket from her past with an unknown value to him, and the key to a locked book she knew would have answers to some questions she had forgotten, maybe even her identity. Her eyes smile at the thought, before focusing again on the VIP table. First she needs to complete her obligation and honor the deal. This last little bit is almost in her grasp.

She waits, watching and fiddling with the pouch for about an hour as the celebration shifts and spreads back out into the tavern. A few of the patrons have already cleared out, heading home or to other engagements. The event is still lively, spread out, festive, but not too out of hand and chaotic. This is the time she wants, the chance for her to return that hideous coat she was to watch like a good admirer, flattered by the duty he gifted her.

"I'm soo lucky," she states aloud as she approaches the festive table, catching the attention of Pasoka and his entourage, "to have an excuse to actually meet you, Master Pasoka," she says in a soft sweet tone.

She makes sure there is no hint of the sarcasm, though it aches to be released, as she speaks. She holds out his coat, to which he gives a nod of appreciation, taking it, and throws it carelessly on an empty chair next to himself. Tweaking his mustache again, this time accompanied by a wolfish grin, he regards her, looking her over like he was taking measurements or trying to figure her worth in regards to himself.

"Indeed," he finally speaks, continuing on with slightly slurred speech from the multiple rounds of ice wine and ale he had downed, toasting himself. "I'm shure itsh a real delight for you... Yer welcome little girl."

Her eyes smile as her hands glide past the dagger she had hidden on her hip and find purchase on the small green bag. She unties it and pulls it free and sets it on the table.

"Master Pasoka, I've had the delight this evening to be enraptured by your creativity again, and I had been wanting to show appreciation and perhaps spend some time getting to know ya, all about ya." She says with an admiring smile in her eyes.

She goes to speak again but is cut off by Pasoka as he leans forward with a grin, "Oh, but I already know you."

Her head tilts slightly and instinctively. Her hand rests on her hip close to the dagger, but looking as non-threatening as possible, going more for cute and unassuming... her eyes do, however, give away a hint of surprise.

"Yesh, I know you, all about you."

Her voice suddenly matches her surprise and curiosity, "You do? You really know me... please tell me."

Her mind races as she voices the inquiry, perhaps Marwi had given her a gift with this task. Is this celebrity someone who holds a key to a part of who I was or my identity? Why is he looking at me like that? Does he have other abilities I didn't count on? Wait, am I under his sway right now?

This last thought is interrupted by Pasoka's thundering laugh as he addresses those around him. "Thish, folksh, is the usual nobody tryin' to use her eshotic eyes and figure to lure me into a relationship shooo I will gift her with all manner of thingsh."

Again a laugh bursts out into the room, this time from the wanderer. "Really? That's what you got, that's all you got? Me... with you, for what, candy and a realization of low self-esteem and a pile of regret?"

The entourage all go silent as the wanderer sighs to herself and reaches toward the bag on the table. "No, never mind, I'll find another way."

Pasoka's hand shoots out for the bag first. He quickly peeks inside, which makes the wanderer tilt her head in sudden curiosity.

"I gladly acshept yer gift as payment for the joy I gave you, but you've worn out yer welcome. Perhapsh, you'll learn mannersh in the future... Get her out of here. Don't bother being nicesh or gentle with thish trash."

The crowd becomes restless as the mood suddenly shifts, with some patrons moving to get a good view while others are trying to get out of the way. With a snap of Pasoka's portly fingers the well-muscled entourage springs into action. The wanderer goes to dodge out of the way, hoping to duck under the arm of a large patron walking by with a couple of tankards. She soon finds a large hand intercepting her from nowhere, grabbing her by the throat before a fist comes in from behind, hitting her hard in the lower side, knocking the breath out of her. She reels a moment, partly from the pain but also surprised at the speed and agility of these women. She finds herself being picked up, still with a tight grip around her throat, just short of choking her but threatening all the same. Another blow comes to the other side as she is then hoisted above the heads of the crowd. Looking back, she notices Pasoka reaching into the bag and waving at her before looking at the jewel.

"Okay," The wanderer shouts, "I get the idea, just put me down and I'll disappear."

The woman who holds her aloft replies, "Sorry Lass, gotta take out the trash. Fortune doesn't shine on ya tonight."

The wanderer looks forward towards her feet as she is being carried horizontally, she sees the door being opened and then feels the force on her body as the two launch her through it. She tucks a bit and kicks off, finding purchase on one of the women's chests, flipping herself forward to land skidding on her feet outside the tavern. Pulling the hidden dagger stashed on her hip, she wipes one of her fingers down the side of the blade causing it to scream to life like a bird of prey, crackling with amber energy. Expecting a fight, she glares over her shoulder at the Pasoka bodyguard whom she kicked off. The large woman grasps at her chest and begins to charge out the door before she is stopped by the other. The two exchange a few words and then the bodyguard slams the tavern door, leaving the wanderer alone with a couple passersby turning and walking the other way.

Exhaling a held breath, she looks at the brilliant illuminated weapon and holds a finger to the mask over her mouth, shushing it, "Shhh, it's okay, not tonight."

The dagger dims and now looks simply worn and charred. She slips it into its hidden sheath and doubles over, taking a deep breath.

Looking up to the sign, she sighs, "Another tavern I can't visit for a little bit, better make a note, later. Also stay away from fancy sweets." She shakes her head and decides it best to get some distance in case the hired help gets an itch for an actual fight.

"Did it even work?" She mocks herself as she walks through several alleys, "Sorry Marwi, I lost your dumb stone trying to be a clever girl."

After ducking down a few alleys, she sees a familiar sight and ducks into a corner shop she knows well, whose speciality is hand pies.

She approaches the old man at the counter, "Two of whatever you think is best."

The old man gives a toothy grin at the familiar customer. "Ah little one, it's nice to see you."

She stretches a bit, testing her sides, noting the lingering pain with a grumble. "Thank you," she says softly, as she places a few coins in the vendor's hand, who gives her two small warm pies.

She sits at a small table in the corner of the shop and takes a bite of one as she stows away the other, wrapped in another bit of parchment, in the same pouch as her other food. Nice and warm, filled with roast vegetables, with the outer crust having a light taste of buttery sweetness. She savors the flavor and warm hearty scent as she calms herself.

The wanderer continues eating at her low lit table of choice, the perfect spot to watch the door and see passersby as well. After a moment of watchfulness, she finishes her meal and relaxes a bit more, quite sure that she wasn't followed. She pulls out the vial she had stashed away, breathes a small sigh of relief, noting it is intact. She swishes it around and stares a moment before stowing it away. "Still the same."

She gets up and walks up to the counter again, clearing her throat a bit, "Anything ya got that Marwi would want?"

The tall old man leans over and chuckles, "I make pies, with food in 'em, I don't make 'em with hasty promises and bad decisions."

She gives a glance to the side and gives a slight giggle. "Right, how about another one of those ya gave me earlier to take to em? He's gotta eat, right?"

She hands over another few coins and accepts a wrapped pie of the same variety. "Thank you." She gives a wave.

"See you soon," the Pie-maker calls after her as she steps into the street and makes for an alleyway. Gathering the shadows around her, she scans the roads outside the shop and follows a familiar path through the night and the mist to the large solitary building that is the Wonder-works.

Walking up to the front door, the shrouded wanderer pulls the vial out again and looks at it, turning it in what light is available, then sighs and tucks it away again before whispering to herself.

"Nothing, perhaps Pasoka has some counter to the charm like I did, or perhaps he doesn't have the stone, or maybe I'm just too far." She pulls the chain and is granted entry by the machinery as usual.

She is stunned, however, to be met at the front door by Marwi. "Come in, come in, the world need not know our business."

She slides into the antechamber and allows the shadows to go back to their proper place as she lowers her hood. Marwi looks at her expectantly as she tilts her head. "I sent ya no word, you were expecting me, then?"

Marwi gives a scowl, "I know your speed and style and I also know the job. What are you getting at? Are you stalling?"

The woman reaches into a pouch and pulls the wrapped hand pie out and hands it over. "I got ya a pie, they are pretty good. It's still warm."

The long spindly hand accepts the pie and he tucks it away into one of several bags he wears about. "Yes, thank you, I'm sure there is a use for it."

She blinks at him and responds dryly, "You eat it."

The ancient being just ignores the remark and holds his hand out again. "Hand it over then." Taking a deep breath, she fishes the vial out again, takes one final glance at it, and gives it to Marwi with a defeated look.

"What did you do? Why do you look like that?" Marwi reads her eyes quickly and regards the vial.

She shrugs and answers, "He got the stone and bag, maybe there is another way that I could get the memories you were after."

Marwi gives a scowl, "Don't be ridiculous, you brought back the vial. He has the stone, you did the correct thing. Except you got a bit curious."

She looks slightly taken aback, "How do you... I wasn't sure how to use it. It didn't work."

Marwi gives an incredulous look. "What, you were thinking it would light up, change color, or do something obviously magical?"

The wanderer's eyes look pensive and a bit guilty as she is suddenly getting the feeling that she is missing something obvious.

The being pokes toward her strange metallic tattoo and Amber eye. "You, of all people, should understand the hidden and ancient art of Artifice, how much of yourself have you lost?"

The wanderer backs up a step, feeling attacked now. "I retain enough to understand myself and know to be protective. It worked, then."

The Elder smirks, holds up the vial and speaks a few hushed words. The label on the vial suddenly blackens and burns away and reveals an etching underneath. Looking at the etching, the wanderer instantly recognizes the strange markings as a language, though she can't read it. The liquid in the vial shimmers and ripples, various images can be seen within, including one that appears to be an image of herself at a younger age, eating some sort of small sweet and laughing. She stares silently for a moment, mesmerized, until Marwi's gruff voice breaks the silence.

"As you can see, you succeeded, but also tainted the memories a bit." He grumbles to himself. "I will filter it out and we will return your memory at no extra cost, but only because of your speed, and because our arrangement has been satisfactory to this point."

She tilts her head, ready to speak, but is cut off by the elder.

"The job is complete. Our arrangement shall be as well, you have paid your due and I will provide what was agreed upon in a day's time. You are one step closer to the key you seek. Meet the morning after next, my new client will have your payment and that answer I teased, as a bonus."

He holds out his large thin hand and holds a small note out to her. "This is the location."

"Amodin's Garden." She looks at the paper for the fourth or fifth time as she stops in her tracks. The familiar clicks can be heard, letting her know her enchantment has ended, and she looks up to see a small boutique that had just recently opened for the day's business.

She smirks to herself and shrugs, "I guess let's finish this... in a boutique?" She steps in and suddenly feels the need to be quite cautious, as she finds herself surrounded by hanging crystal bottles of various shapes and sizes. The space itself is simple and elegant with various plants placed around the small main room which is designed to look like a garden. She notices a few people marveling and inspecting the bottles, but none that look to be the proprietor.

She walks to the counter and speaks up, "Excuse me."

The other customers look at her and then go about their business, smelling flowers and admiring the bottles. It isn't long before the bright-eyed young owner of the shop pokes their head out from the back. Their hair is short and bright white, matching the smile on their ageless face. Shimmering yellow-green eyes suddenly smile to her in recognition.

"You are here because you helped a mutual benefactor," a calm clear voice speaks, almost washing away the wanderer's nervousness. "You helped them, and so you helped me, and I thank you."

They slide an envelope across the counter, "I believe this is a key that you had lost. Oh, and I have more. Would you like to see what you helped create? My special new creation, the first of many to come."

The shop owner urges the wanderer to follow them behind the counter to another room, also full of hanging crystal bottles, but much smaller and all empty. They lead to one larger one in particular which almost seems to glow a warm white light.

The shop owner holds the bottle toward her and nods. The girl gives a questioning look, "What is it?"

Amodin, the shop owner smiles, "I make the scents of memories. With your help I made this one, full of inspiration, excitement and childhood delight." They open the bottle and a fragrance wafts into the air.

The wanderer breathes in lightly and finds the scent to be sweet, like a delicious dessert, bringing feelings of excited joy, like during holidays, or relishing exotic delights. She feels herself start to get swept up in the emotions, but then the burning pain in her eye pulls her free again as she blinks away a few tears.

"It's what we took..."

The figure quickly and gently corrects the wanderer, "It is what you reclaimed for our benefactor that marked the end of a previous agreement that was abandoned by the deal breaker. Yes, I used a bit of that memory, childish delight and the magic it held. Thanks to your help this is but the first of a series of collaborations with Marwi and myself."

The wanderer nods, "Thank ya for satisfying my curiosity. Other than the key, Marwi said he would recover something else for me that I had lost."

Amodin nods and pulls a tiny crystal tincture bottle from their pocket. "This is a scent only for you, its smell is quite sweet, and it is fleeting, but the memory is yours to keep once again."

The wanderer grips the tiny bottle in her hand and starts to make her way out of the shop, grabbing the envelope and tucking it away as she passes it.

She stops and looks back to regard Amodin who followed her out, "Best fortune to you and your lovely scents. A bit of advice?" The shop owner smiles and nods, awaiting it.

"Always make sure you keep your end." Amodin smiles and nods in agreement as the Wanderer walks outside, a key to her identity resting inside an envelope in one pocket, the perfume holding a childhood memory of sweet things in another, and the City of Destiny in front of her.

Nose Candy
Edward Palmer

Just after my mentor stopped calling me apprentice, I still found myself struggling to fully understand what I was capable of. An opportunity presented itself to learn more about myself and the world around me. Being an alchemist had so far been studying books, I was not going to get access to any special laboratories until I had proven myself. This is how I found myself sitting in a gray car under a cold gray sky with an old graying man. We were at a bus station several miles between any major cities. There are a few things he wants to tell me about what is expected out of me tonight.

Don't be a hero." I don't think it's a coincidence he started with this. "Keep one eye on the bags, and another eye on everything else." The old man let out a sound that could have been a chuckle once. "I know it seems like a waste of your time, but it's important work. If you find yourself nodding off, do whatever you have to do to keep focused." I started to get out of his car. "Last reminder do not use any real names. Not yours, not any organization, and don't take this the wrong way but I don't want to know anything about you."

Despite the warmth shown, I kept everything he said in mind. This was my first assignment on my own, I didn't want to screw it up. It was simple enough to understand. Ensuring that certain bags get picked up when they are supposed to be. I'm not to talk to anybody. That means nobody handling the bags, nobody that works at the bus lines, and certainly no cops or other authority figures. It's weird but this courier service has been going since the 90's, so whatever. Job pays well. I also only had to work one or two shifts a month, for a lazy guy like me it helps.

There's nothing illegal going on here, not with the bags anyway. They aren't the only reason I'm doing this. The world is a more dangerous place than most people realize, even as bad as things might be.

Legitimate monsters prey on the less fortunate, and have an easier time blending in at places like this. This is difficult for me to understand, so I try not to think too much about it. From what I have been told, there are other worlds than ours. It is easier to cross from our world to theirs in luminal places. I'm not even sure what I'm looking for here, it's a 'know it when you see it' type of deal.

My shift comes and goes. All the bags I had to take note of went out and nobody seems to care that I was there for 12 hours. Most of the time was spent tapping away at my netbook, pretending to wait for somebody. I do have a knack for being overlooked.

During a bathroom break near the end of the night a young man approached me as I was washing my hands. "Could you help me, Mr.?" He asked nervously, "I want to get rid of this stuff and get home?" He had two little bags filled with a white powder. I bought them mainly to help the kid out, also if I must do this type of thing, I might be able to find other uses for this besides staying awake.

. . . .

AFTER A FEW MONTHS, this becomes an easy routine. Black bag with red stripes leaves at 9, green bag with white stripes arrives at 10. Everything gets loaded and picked up, I'm just here to watch. Since it's a good idea to rotate us, I have had the pleasure of visiting several different stations in the region. Of course, they started off all looking alike, so it can be a little disconcerting trying to remember where you are.

Other people here vary little as well. Most of them are just trying to get to somewhere else or help someone do the same. Sometimes you get a more nefarious asshole there to see if there are any prey about. I try to keep an eye on them. So far I had not seen anything that wasn't human.

I'm not the only one out here keeping a watch. There are other groups trying to keep humanity safe. Information about these other groups is sketchy. One of them likes to pretend they are suit and tie wearing government agents. Supposedly they aren't as violent towards us as they used to be. At least I hope the one walking towards me isn't.

"Waiting for someone, friend?" This was my cue to leave, so I started getting up.

"Nope, I must have missed him." He did nothing to impede me. Stopping short, the man in the dark suit looked toward the exit.

"I'm not here to stop you, and I don't care about your bags. We should talk, not here, of course." Making my way now, after I had a pause that seemed to go on for way too long.

"I don't know what you are talking about." The exit seemed to stay the same distance even as I started to hurry my pace.

"I believe you. At least, I believe you don't know why you are really here." Isn't it the worst when some ass makes a decent point like that? "We can get that sorted out, at least you won't have to be here like bait."

After what seemed like an hour of walking I made it through the door. It's a few months before I get contacted again. As a precaution the bosses make sure the bad guys aren't trying to get to me, but I'm pretty sure it goes the other way too. Best use of the time is to figure out a way to sense them before they can sense me, sniff them out if you will.

· · · ·

"DIFFERENT SORT OF SITUATION tonight kid, don't worry about the bags, they have been taken care of. Something happened earlier, something bad." He never gave me a chance to ask what happened but got this out in a nerve fueled rant. "None of ours got hurt, and we're going to keep it that way. We need you to take a look around and come right back out. I should warn you, your agent friend might be in there. You do not want to be in a room alone with him, am I clear?"

After I answered him, we watched an ambulance leave followed by a few cop cars. "Give me a minute, I forgot something in my car." He shrugged as he pulled away. What I forgot were the baggies I picked up on my first night. I found a way to modify them, should make it easier for me to sense other denizens in the night. Not just monsters either, but my buddy in the suit too. I take a quick bump, after making sure nobody was looking. Think of it as reinterpreting the secrets of the ancients for modern living. Another bump just to be sure.

The process I used turned the high into more of a focusing of my senses. Nothing seemed to have changed, at least not immediately. I probably should have tested it before tonight, but live and learn. The lights in the station weren't any different than the other nights, for some reason I was expecting them to become brighter or something. I could see a security guard heading back to his office. A strong antiseptic smell was coming from his direction.

Now I could see my Mr. Agent, he was paying a lot of attention to his phone. It wouldn't have been too hard to pick him out, he had to be the only person wearing shades in the middle of the night. Must have alerted him, he jerked his head up. Luckily, I averted my eyes at the last second. For some reason, that seemed like a good idea.

"You again." He began to get up, putting his phone away in a smooth motion. "I'm actually kind of glad you are here." My hand covered my mouth mocking a surprised gesture and began walking toward the back of the station. If he's behind me, it's not like I can get jumped by anything worse. Well hopefully not.

Yellow tape hung limply across the entrance to an area with an old flickering television and vending machines. There was still a bucket filled with grey water, the floor was almost done drying. I kept walking. Another room was beyond this one, filled with lockers and chairs. The lights were usually off in these types of spaces.

As I approached, I could already smell something off, coming from a dark corner. First it seemed like an older type of perfume, flowers dipped in alcohol type of scent. But it changed, as if it were covering up a much more horrible stench. A shit stink, like old sweat and leather filled my nostrils. I tried to keep myself from reacting too strongly. I pulled out my phone, using it as a light source.

"Do you smell that perfume?" I wasn't sure how close the Agent was until he spoke. Ahead of us was what appeared to be an old person, a woman if I had to guess. She was covered in old flannels and filthy blankets. Her hair was a tangle of white and gray wisps. What little I could see of her skin was wrinkled and mottled. She was having a conversation with a rat, making squeaking noises with her mouth, which still had a bit of dried blood next to it.

The rat squealed in surprise and took off, running off to a hole in a nearby wall. The woman, I was becoming less convinced of just what she was the longer I looked, also cried out at the sight of us. She ran at a speed that would be impossible to a metal security door flinging it open. If it weren't for the clang it made in protest, I would not have believed the door to have been locked. She continued running into wherever it led.

The Agent was just as shocked as I was. It seemed I recovered first and turned around, back to the entrance. "We need to come up with a plan." He started.

"Don't worry buddy, I already got one in the car." I answered as I exited as fast as I could.

Nose Candy

V.R. Leavitt

I love my human. She loves me. I am a dog, so what's not to love? My human also has a cat, who I do not love, but sometimes she likes to try to cuddle with me, which my human thinks is cute, but I get anxious about it because of that time that the cat smacked me in the face. My human said I might have deserved it after chasing the cat under the bed, but the cat should have better manners. I thought she wanted to play. I was wrong, apparently. The cat sends mixed signals. I'm just a simple dog, so I don't always understand. And even though I don't love the cat a whole lot, I love to go in the cat's box and snack on what she leaves in there and I have no idea why. Neither does my human, but the cat seems to think it's funny.

We live in a building with other humans. Some of them have dogs because I get to see them when my human takes me out for walks. We usually go for a nice walk in the mornings before my human goes to work, and another one in the evening when she gets home. I love walks. My human likes to take me to the dog park on the days she doesn't work, and on the way home we go to the coffee place and she gets something for her and I get something for me, which I love! When we're in the drive-in, the smells coming through the window are amazing. I love to smell all the different smells, except there's one I don't like, but I don't know what it is because again, I'm just a simple dog. It smells like something my human puts in her tea sometimes when she has that instead of coffee. I think it's called lemon, and it smells like trash, but worse, because I actually like the smell of trash, because it has all kinds of yummy things in it like meat scraps and other scraps that my human won't let me have. She really didn't like it when I pulled the trash onto the floor one day when she was at work so I could check it all out and I don't know why because there's just *so much to smell* inside the trash! I got in trouble for that one, and again, the cat thought it was funny.

My human likes to smell things too. Maybe she's a dog too, just a different type of dog. She has bottles of perfume, brings fresh flowers home from the store, and even lights smelly candles sometimes. She also makes food which has all kinds of smells, and she always takes a nice deep sniff of her food before she eats it. Some of these smells are okay, but they are not all my favorites. She likes them though. One time the cat singed her whiskers in one of the candle flames, which *I* thought was funny.

One day recently, my human started to stay at home, which I thought was great! I don't like when she goes to work all day. But she seemed upset for some reason. We would still go on walks, but she would wear this thing on her face when we'd go out. And instead of her going out on the weekend to bring home food, somebody brought the food to our house. They also had a thing on their face. My human also started rubbing this very stinky goo on her hands. Like a lot of it. Things are different now, and I don't know why, but I don't think it's really great. In fact, I'm pretty sure it's not good at all.

Today, when we were still snuggled in bed, before she got up, my human felt very warm. Not like a good warm, like she normally feels, but a bad warm. She also smelled different, like a smell I've never smelled before. She's been sick before, but this was different. When she woke up, she took me out, but just for a quick walk, not even our usual walk which is also how I know something is wrong. She opened my bag of treats and put her nose in it. The look on her face was not good. She gave me a treat, but then opened one of her smelly candles and smelled it. She also tried to smell her bouquet of flowers, but she just kept getting more and more upset. She went to the bathroom and put that little stick thing in her mouth that makes the beeps. It beeped a lot, and she made a phone call and went back to bed. I went with her. The cat had never left the bed, but that's not unusual. My human slept for a lot of that day. And the next day.

The day after that she got up and made some food, and sat on the couch and put on the TV. Something big is happening since on the TV the guy talks about the same thing over and over again. My human tried eating her food. She took a nice big sniff of her food, but then she started crying. She laid down on the couch. It's not a big couch so I couldn't lay with her, but I put my head on the couch next to her. She was still crying, but she pet my head and rubbed my ears. I don't know how to help her, so I just try to be near her. The cat must think something is wrong too because the cat has been near her a lot as well. My human seems so sad, I wish I could help.

One day, in the morning, we went on another very, very short walk. My human is now barking, which she doesn't normally do. This afternoon she put a pad down for me which normally means she has to work late, but she hasn't been working at all. She just sleeps, and now barks as she tries to sleep. But the pad means we're not going for a walk later.

The pads continued for a few days, which made me sad because I do love walks and the dog park, but also because it means my human is not here. Of course, she *is* here, but not really. The barking has slowed down, but it's still there. She makes a scary sound when she sleeps too. She still gets sad when she tries to smell her food, and she doesn't eat very much of it anyway. She watches TV and cries a lot. She talks to other humans on the phone, and cries some more. The cat and I try to keep her company as best we can. This is the longest stretch I can remember of the cat not being a jerk to me. But nothing feels right and I wonder if things will ever go back to normal again.

Then one day, my human woke up and went into the kitchen to make her morning drink. She smelled the jar like she always does but still looked sad. But that day she made her morning food, and ate it all. Then she got washed up, and took me for a walk! An actual walk! It wasn't as long as our normal walks, but not a short walk either. It was fantastic. It was great to smell all the smells around us, like the flowers, the other animals on walks, the humans, the weird but yummy smell of the food cart guy. It was amazing. I was sad when we had to go back inside, but at least it was a walk finally. My human put a pad down again though and went right to bed when we got back.

Slowly, my human started barking less and being awake more, which was good! We even started going on walks consistently at least once a day which was even better. She started making more food, and eating it more too. She would still take her big sniff of it each time though and get a little sad. Could she not smell it? Everything she made smelled good to me, well most of it. She made something with lemon in it and I stayed far away. I felt sad for her. Smelling is the best thing in the world! I love smells! She loves smells too, but what if she couldn't smell anymore? That seemed pretty terrible. In the meantime, I was just glad she seemed to be more back to normal. She still wore the thing on her face if somebody came to the door, to deliver the food, and she still stayed home instead of going to work, but the barking had pretty much stopped and she didn't sleep all day. And did I mention walks? We walked more and more each day which made me very, very happy.

Then, one day, we woke up. My human gave me some nice long scratches before she got out of bed. I followed her into the kitchen. So did the cat. We sat and waited for our treats and our food. And then my human opened her jar of morning drink powder and gave it a sniff. She started crying again, but this time it was different. She seemed happy. She grabbed a candle and sniffed it, she opened other containers of food and sniffed them, each time getting more and more excited. If she had a tail she would have been wagging it like crazy, I'm sure. She sat down on the floor next to me and the cat, still crying, but in that happy way, and hugged us both. It was a good day. I knew things were finally going to be all right.

Nose Candy

Christoph Bruce

"**B**ecause, I don't like wearing it!"

Massimo wasn't sure who he was replying to, or why he had said what he had said.

What perplexed Massimo the most was that he couldn't remember what he had just been thinking about, and that disturbed him. At a loss, he dropped to one knee.

Pain threatened to overtake him. Was it pain, or, was it pleasure? There was sweetness all around him. His mind was trying to stay afloat, but he knew in his bones that he was failing.

A beautiful and familiar voice penetrated the honeyed porridge, "No no, don't even think about getting up. You just lie there."

Massimo was instantly reoriented. There was cool grass on his naked ass and shoulder blades, and Dzifa was straddling him. The pleasure-pain was gone, but he could still smell something sweet and perverse. The smell was wrong, of course. The scent of the woman who was controlling him at her leisure was one that Massimo was well familiar with, and lacked the will to forget.

With one skilled slide, Dzifa caused Massimo's eyes to pop wide open at his mind's screaming of impending orgasm.

"Not, yet Massi." Dzifa hissed as her next move brought him back from the edge.

A shuddering wave through his spine closed Massimo's eyes. He hated being called "Massi." Through the course of his primary and secondary schooling, Massimo had served two suspensions from school and another twenty-six days in after school detention for violence that he had delivered to boys who had dared to call him "Massi." Those boys clearly lacked the angelic beauty and sheer pelvic floor power that Dzifa used to put him in his place.

Massimo opened his eyes to see the beautiful woman with the cocky smile over him. He was once again struggling to stay afloat. This time it was love that was attempting to hold his head underwater. Dzifa was his third, first real girlfriend. She was the first person with whom he had made true love where sex and intimacy melded together. From on his back, Massimo was enthralled by her breast bouncing playfully and the halo of the sun's rays around her hair. He was afraid that he'd finish himself off should he make eye-contact.

Massimo's thoughts were interrupted when Dzifa asked, "Why aren't you wearing protection?"

"Are you worried about other girls' diseases or getting pregnant?" Massimo said this with a wry smile. Humor being the supreme defense mechanism.

"Not that protection. Your mask." Dzifa looked so full of sorrow. "You need to learn to be safe."

"What are you◇" His query was interrupted upon stubbing his toe and smacking face first into the ground.

Massimo's sinuses and throat were full of what seemed to be a sickly honey powder. He must have been breathing it off the ground. But, why was he there? Had he been walking?

"Midshipman, are you paying attention?" a bassy voice cut in.

From his desk, Massimo looked over to the instructional screen and to Captain Mercer.

"Well, Midshipman...Principino, is it?" Mercer would always use that trick on new students. He would look down at the roll and use a perfect pause between 'Midshipman' and your name to give the impression that he was trying to determine if it would be to his advantage to learn your name or not. But, Massimo didn't know why Mercer was talking to him like that. He and Mercer had known each other the whole time he'd been at the Academy, and the Captain usually called him "Massimo". Though, Massimo guessed that Mercer wouldn't have called him that in our first class together.

This was all irritatingly surpassing Massimo's rational capability. How could he have a first time meeting with someone that he already knew to be his mentor? Also, why was Mercer wearing his dress uniform with full regalia? The medals bouncing and the cutlass slapping his leg as he lectured were a tad distracting.

"Shall I repeat the question, Midshipman Principino?" Mercer asked with an expert grumble. "What does the phrase "Comfort kills" mean to you?"

The knowledge that he was now at parade rest listening to a mission briefing prevented Massimo from answering.

"Have you had a chance to review all of your mission objectives and each objective's accompanying protocols?" the Commodore said in a 'you have to eat all of your peas before you get any ice cream' tone.

Masimo was very familiar with the Commodore. She was a middle aged woman with graying hair that cut a rather authoritative image in an Exploration Command uniform.

As to her question, "Yes, Commodore." Massimo reflexively replied in a 'these peas will sprout and grow to a size that would allow me to fight a fucking giant before I'd eat them' tone.

The Commodore followed with an overly dramatic staged tilting of her head to let Massimo know that she was ever so mildly annoyed with him. "Lt. Commander Principino, every Mission Specialist must have planning and review meetings with their Command Authority Officer before they go on any solo mission," she said flatly. Maintaining the same tone, "It should make no difference that *your* Command Authority Officer is your mother."

After a long smirk, Massimo responded, "I'm good at what I do, Mother."

"Good nothing! You're the best in the whole fleet, you little smirking asshole!"

There she was! Massimo's smirk blossomed into a devilish smile.

Admitting a small defeat the Commodore exhaled a phenomenon that was equal parts sigh and chuckle. "Massimo, you're very good, but you're not perfect. One of these days, your disregard for protocol could prove catastrophic."

"I know." Massimo meets her halfway, "I'll do better. I promise."

"Thank you."

Through a loving smile, Massimo said, "Calling me an asshole was a bit rough."

His mother rolls her eyes. "It just seemed less mal à propos than calling you a little cocksucker."

"Your maternal instincts are on point." Laughing, Massimo released his arms from parade rest to give her a hug. Once again, he tripped on a tree root and fell flat on his face.

"Momodore, why is there a root in this conference ro..." Before he'd even finished the sentence, Massimo knew that he wasn't in the conference room any more.

"Did you hear what I said, Massimo?"

Fuck, thought Massimo. I'm going to look up and see Lee Zollman leaning on the Rainbow Gum Eucalyptus Tree.

Zollman, feeling that he was repeating himself, said, "I said that we're all mulch in the end."

Massimo was growing angry that Zollman wasn't helping him up. He started to get up to tell him so, but found that he was already leaning against the Gum with Lee. They were in the Native Plant Collection at the International Students Academy in Jakarta. The Gum had been their favorite tree to bullshit under. There was also a corpse flower nearby which normally stinks up the area with the smell of death, but today it smelled oddly sweet.

Lee chided, "You should be wearing your mask. Why aren't you?"

"Because, I don't like wearing it!" Massimo continued angrily, "I'd already answered you."

But, Massimo started to wonder if he had. He felt like he had said that, but he didn't remember who he had been answering. Massimo felt awash in discomfort.

"Comfort kills!" boomed the bassy voice from seemingly nowhere.

Not knowing where the voice called from, all Massimo could do was let out a defeated and agitated, "What?"

Choosing to ignore Massimo's tone, Lee asks, "Are you still leaving Jakarta after this semester?"

"Yes."

"Heading off to Space Camp?"

Now, it is Massimo's turn to ignore tone. "I'll spend two years at the Old Academy in Annapolis. If I pass that, I'll be transferred to the Titan Orbiting Deep Launch Station to complete my training."

"So, you really want to be an explorer?" Lee managed to say "explorer" as if Massimo had told him that he wanted to be a ninja.

"Yes. I want to make a difference."

"Ha, make a difference. If you'd study philosophy you'd know that we're all mulch in the end. All our beliefs, purposes, and attempts to make a difference are all just attempts to mask us from the smell."

Indignity was welling up in Massimo. Why is everyone bringing up masks? Turning indignity to rage, Massimo felt his anger veering towards Zollman.

"You've never taken a single philosophy class in your life. You merely possess a fortune cookie level understanding of Eastern Religions!" was the barb Massimo flung back.

"Well the First-Year curriculum for physics is very difficult. In fact, it's so arduous that…"

"…that many students drop out." Massimo finished that often repeated line for him.

"Indeed," Lee said, not allowing Massimo to steal his thunder. "It's jokingly referred to as pre-business, because most students drop it and end up in business school."

"You may have mentioned that little factoid once or twice before."

"Well, it's true. So, I'll start taking philosophy courses with gusto when my Third-Year elective slots open up."

Lee changed the subject, "Anyway, I have a new girlfriend."

"Does she know?" Massimo's agitated state couldn't help but chime in. His consciousness was blurring. The non-corpse smell of the corpse flower had become overpowering.

"Of course! Well, mostly. Her name is Dzifa. We're in the early chill phase, but I think that we both know that it's real. Oh, you'll love her! She's a knockout, Massimo."

Massimo could still hear Lee talking, but he couldn't focus enough to follow along.

"But, don't get any funny ideas, because she'd never go for an adventure boy like you."

Massimo's head was in honey, again. He struggled to pull himself back to focus. His mind was swimming, and there was a sickly sweetness washing over him.

The soft grass was back on Massimo's ass, and he felt Dzifa grinding on top of him.

Massimo couldn't deny the cliché as he exclaimed, "I could die here."

"It's certainly a weird time to talk of death, Midshipman!" the bassy voice boomed.

Massimo's eyes jolted open to see the fully uniformed and mustachioed Mercer bouncing up and down.

"What the Fuck?!?"

"Language, Midshipman," Mercer scolded as his medals bounced and his cutlass slapped on Massimo's outer thigh. "One *must* keep a level of professionalism in every affair."

"Yes, sir!" Massimo blurted out while trying to stand at attention on his back.

"Is he wearing his protective gear," the familiar and disapproving female voice chimed in.

"No, Commodore, he is not."

Dzifa added, "This could be us, Massi."

Massimo looks over to see Dzifa with Zollman's arm around her shoulders. He is frozen on the ground with his gaze moving back and forth between Mercer and Dzifa as his mouth hangs agape.

"Dzifa, why would I want this?" Massimo pleaded. "How could you even begin to imagine that I'd want him instead of you?"

A supremely disappointed Commodore whispers under her breath, "He's disrespecting a superior officer right in front of his own mother."

Ignoring his mother, Massimo could do nothing but look pleadingly at Dzifa.

"But, you did pick him!"

"Dzifa, I...AAAAAA!"

Massimo's world exploded in pain! Dzifa shimmered in front of his eyes before changing into first a vision of his mother and then into nothingness.

Something had pierced through his right leg. The only possibility that presented itself was that Mercer had come down at a bad angle and his cutlass had stabbed Massimo's leg. He opened his eyes to plead for Mercer to get off of him, but Mercer wasn't there. In fact no one was there.

Realizing that he was standing, Massimo looked down to see if he could pull the cutlass out of his leg. Only there was no cutlass. What he saw was what appeared to be a long, smooth wooden spike which had pierced completely through both his Exploration Command Environmental Protection Suit and his leg.

"That looks like it hurts."

Massimo looked up to see Zollman leaning up against the Gum in the Native Plant Collection. Only, he realized that the plants were wrong.

"How's the smell?"

"Fuck off, Lee!"

But, Lee was gone. All Massimo could see were the wrong plants. He caught motion out of the corner of his eye, but it was too late.

"AAAAA!"

Two new points of pain seared through Massimo's left leg. He looked down to see the second and third spikes that had torn holes in his suit.

Through all the pain, Massimo had a profound realization. "My suit!"

Massimo's hands shoot up to his helmet to notify his ship that he needed emergency assistance. Then, his heart sank. There was nothing where the panic button should be. He wasn't wearing his mask.

"Comfort kills, my boy."

Two more impacts thudded into Massimo, but there was next to no pain this time. He didn't need to look to see that one spike had gone into his ribcage just under his right arm while the second one had pierced through his neck from the left.

"I tried to warn you, Massi."

Massimo looked up wanting to see Dzifa's beautiful eyes one more time, but it was his mother's eyes that waited for him.

"I'm sorry," was all that Massimo could say.

As the sickly sweetness washed over him, Massimo witnessed the vision of his mother morph into Dzifa, then Mercer, then Dzifa once more.

Massimo wanted to scream at each of them for help, but when his lips parted all the came out was a quiet, "I'm sorry."

The last fear that grasped Massimo was the terror that these dear visions didn't know what they meant to him. He wanted to tell them everything.

"I'm sorry." came out as a whisper that no human ear could hear.

"I'm sorry."

Consciousness was no longer a gift bestowed upon Massimo Principino.

• • • •

THE PLANT THAT HAD entrapped its first human had never possessed anything resembling consciousness. There was no knowledge of humanity. It did not know that it was what humans called a plant that had trigger-hairs that activated rigid spiky outer guard-hairs or a pitcher body.

However, it didn't need to know anything to begin to break down its latest catch. No thought was necessary for the prey to be broken down into energy for its growth, shredded mulch to protect its roots, and the next several waves of sweet smelling pheromones.

• • • •

SITTING ON A SMALL hilltop overlooking a forested hollow is the Exploration Command SE-077. The small ship is in energy-save mode. This occurs when the ship's sole operator hasn't attempted to use any of its functions for an extended period of time. SE-077's operator hadn't attempted to do anything since he had exited the craft eighty-three hours ago. The ship's interior is completely dark with the exception of a small flashing green light on the communication console. In its attempt to inform anyone that a communique had arrived, the little green light does little to brighten the ship, but it does rhythmically reflect on and off on the face mask of the Exploration Command Environmental Protection Suit sitting unused on the console.

The following communique is now waiting in the communication console memory.

Dear Massimo,

You'll be getting an official communique here shortly, but I thought that I'd go ahead and reach out to you first.

The reports that you've sent back have us all very excited. Based on your preliminary findings and safety checks, Exploration Command has decided to send a Secondary Survey Team.

In non-EC news, Dzifa, and her businessman husband Lee, just had their first child. This could be *your* happy moment. I'm just saying... I know that you don't like me getting involved, but she loved you a lot. Can't you learn to open up? You need to stop thinking of women as Venus Fly Traps.

Sorry to complain. This should be a happy occasion.

Good work,

Commodore Principino

P.S. I swear I'm too formal for my own good. I seriously just signed off on a personal letter to my son as "Commodore".

Sorry, sweetie. You really have done a great job, and I'm proud of you.

Keep it up, you little cocksucker!

It really looks like that, thanks to your work, the research team will be walking into a picnic.

Love,

Mom

Nose Candy

Lucy Waterson

• • • •

I SMELL HIM BEFORE I see him. The acrid tang of woodsmoke fills the air and I can feel my throat constrict, so much so I have to sit down.

He smiles as he walks past, possibly wondering why I am panting slightly. I watch as he strides across the floor towards the bar. He is obviously well known here. Numerous people call out as he walks past and he greets them all with a raised hand or a nod of the head. He has friends.

He is shorter than average with wide shoulders. The impression of a triangle walking on its point is not an easy image to dispel from my mind. His hair is dark and straight, although the ends that brush the collar of his shirt curl ever so slightly. His clothes are unremarkable, but I suspect that may be the point.

I lose sight of him when he gets to the bar and I turn back to my book, trying to concentrate on the words on the page rather than the scene around me.

The bar isn't busy. There are maybe twenty people in the whole place and I don't suppose I am doing a good job of blending in, seeing as how I am on my own. But the miasma of smells around me is both intoxicating and off-putting. Sweat, cologne, perfume, all hang in the air above my head. Swirling ribbons of scent that if I concentrate I can actually see.

The woman standing by the jukebox is chewing peppermint flavoured gum. There is a waft of mint every time she opens her mouth.

I can smell the alcohol as well. Smells rich enough to make me a little unsteady on my feet, and the reason why I am drinking water, still, not sparkling.

The strongest scent of all, over all of the others, is the thread of woodsmoke that blew in with the latest arrival. It is irritating and I have to lay my book down on the table to cover my mouth while I cough.

"*Great Expectations*."

And there he is, smiling at me. Breathing is harder now and, to be perfectly honest, I probably should have left the moment he walked in, this is a last resort after all, but it is too late now and I am committed.

He has a glass in one hand. A pint of bitter, the smell of it rises upwards and joins the many others swirling around my head.

"One of Dickens's better novels," I reply, a little breathlessly.

As he sits down, thankfully for my sanity, on the other side of the table, I notice his eyes are grey, like the smell that surrounds him and that I am struggling to see past.

"I would have thought you'd have preferred Jane Austen. *Persuasion*, perhaps?"

"Actually I prefer *Pride and Prejudice*."

He winks at me as though he's just caught me out and I probably should have smiled back at him, but the woodsmoke is collecting at the back of my throat, and I cough instead. I am quietly impressed by the fact that he doesn't flinch, most people would have. And in fact a woman sitting two tables away does turn to glare at me. I raise my hand in a salute and she immediately turns away.

He sips at his drink and I watch him. He doesn't seem at all worried by my presence which I find interesting. But eventually I get bored.

"Do you know why books smell?"

"Do I lose points if I say no?"

I consider the question and then shake my head.

"In that case, no, I don't know why books smell."

I look down at my copy of *Great Expectations* and smile. "Books are made from paper and adhesive. As they age they release organic volatile compounds scented with just a hint of vanilla."

"Actually I hate the way books smell." He smiles at me as though he's won.

The odour of woodsmoke is getting stronger now and all the other smells seem to be intensifying as well. If I stay here much longer I will have a headache, and then my concentration will slip, and this bar is too crowded to let that happen.

So, I stand up, put my book into my large shoulder bag, and leave the bar. His eyes track me as I go.

Outside the sun has gone. The sky is doubtless peppered by stars, but I can't actually see any of them thanks to the bright lights that illuminate the car park.

I move away from the building. The air around me is no longer cloying and heavy with the scent of people. There are other scents instead, the biggest one being the tang of diesel and motor oil from the parked cars. It makes my nose itch. Best of all is the indefinable night-time smell, clearing out my sinuses and making me breathe deeply, until that is the tang of woodsmoke takes over once again.

I swivel back towards the building. He's standing in a pool of light and I can see him quite clearly. To him I must be an indistinct blur, my edges bleeding into the night.

"You didn't tell me your name," he complains.

The aggrieved tone of his voice makes me laugh.

"What's so funny?"

I step forward into the light so he can see me.

"What is this obsession with names?" I am standing half in half out of the pool of light. I let go of the control I have been holding in place and my features twist on my face. Brown eyes turn blue, a petite nose gets larger and longer, my ears stick out from my head just a fraction more than before, and my hair, dark blonde styled in a choppy pixie cut, which I rather like, grows longer and greyer.

"I'm not obsessed." He sounds defensive now, and he takes a step forward, closer to me. I step back. "I just would really like to know the name of the woman I'll be waking up next to in the morning."

That statement makes me laugh again. I think he really means it.

"C'mon," he croons, as though I can be cajoled into complying. As though his words will be enough to make me change my mind, but my mind was made up even before I set eyes on him. "It'd be great, really great. And wasn't that what the whole pantomime with the books was about?"

His impertinence surprises me. I should finish this now before he gets any further ideas. I've been around for a very long time and it's rare that I meet a man who isn't prepared to take what he wants.

"No, it wasn't."

He doesn't believe my words. I don't need to see his face to know that.

"Is that any way to talk to your future husband?"

"You're a fast mover." I can smell the desire coming off him. I decide to step forwards. Let him get a proper look at my face.

His eyes widen in shock and disbelief, and I see him glance over his shoulder as though he thinks he is being observed, but there is nobody else out here.

"You've been lighting fires, haven't you?" Now he's seen what he's seen there's no point holding back any more.

"Me?" He does a good innocent act, but I can smell the lie.

"Lighting fires for fun." I smile and he smiles back. Perhaps he imagines us as co-conspirators, plotting together.

He shrugs. "It's not like anyone gets hurt. I'm always careful."

And he is. Never starting a fire too close to a populated area, and creating a fire break before he starts.

"It's art," he states clearly, his eyes gleam. "But from the look of you I don't think you'd understand."

"And what about all the animals that you kill and the plants? Are their deaths part of the art too?"

He takes a step towards me. He seems to have got over his reluctance to get too close. I could almost admire him for that.

"Nobody cares about a few plants and animals." He's confident now, grinning at me. He reaches out and although I move away I'm not fast enough and he manages to grab hold of my arm. His hold on it is tight enough to leave bruises.

"I care," I tell him, but he just grins and tightens his grip. "I was going to give you a chance," I say. "A chance to apologise, a chance to make amends."

He laughs at me. He laughs for a long time. "You? *You* were going to give *me* a chance?"

I reach out with my left arm, the one he's not holding, and curl my fingers.

"Yes," I say, keeping my eyes fixed on his face. "I was."

Then I stretch my fingers out straight and I am alone. Just the merest hint of woodsmoke dissipating into the night air.

Lucy Waterson is a writer based in Southampton, England. She is the mother of three boys and has a degree in archaeology. Over the last five years she has had over 30 stories published, most in short story anthologies. Last year one of her stories was published by Tyche Books in an anthology titled 'Water: Selkies, Sirens, and Sea Monsters'. This book has won the Douglas Barbour Award for Speculative Fiction from the Book Publishers Association of Alberta. Her favourite genres to write and read are fantasy and crime fiction, and it was drawing on ideas from both that led her to create the Anwich City Watch. She is currently writing a novel (provisionally titled The Truth Seer) in which both Raoul and Cade have starring roles. You can find her on Facebook as Lucy Waterson Author.

· · · · ·

ANDREW BENSON BROWN is a Missouri-based poet and journalist. He is the author of the mock-epic poem Legends of Liberty, a series-in-progress that, when complete, will dramatize the full arc of the American Revolution. His poems, essays, and reviews have appeared in Asses of Parnassus, Sparks of Calliope, Scarlet Leaf Review, Compulsive Reader, New Book Review, The Society of Classical Poets, and other journals. He is a history writer for American Essence magazine and contributes to The Epoch Times, writing articles for the Life and Tradition, and Arts and Culture sections. He is an editor at Bard Owl Publishing and Communications. For more information about his projects and to check out his literature blog, go to http://apollogist.word-press.com.

· · · ·

HUMPHREY PRIMP has had an ongoing interest in providing art and writing to some of David J. Knight's various publications; namely the art zine *XAGGERA* (Fenylalanine Publishing 2016), *Tales of a Guelphite*, and a few other Fenylalanine publications (*FPP2, FPP3* 2017) See the Fenylalanine Publishing site at: https://fenylalanine.wordpress.com

Primp generally works solo.

Johanna A. Fromond has been mentioned in the comic *Tales of a Guelphite #3* (Fenylalanine Publishing 2021).

Fromond generally works solo.

Any Second is Fromond and Primp's first collaboration, apparently inspired by a canoe trip not so very long ago along the Speed River in Guelph, Ontario, Canada.

• • • •

CRAFTED JUST OUTSIDE of Washington D.C., **Michael Lauria** has been daydreaming ever since. He has been wandering at times and experiencing different events and settings throughout his life weaving stories along the way. After embarking on a couple adventures in Brazil, he finds himself currently tucked away in Kannapolis, North Carolina, telling exciting stories fueled by artisanal coffee and imagining the next major adventure. You can follow him, and discover his works via http://Twitter.com/ImaginaryLauria

• • • •

EDWARD PALMER, Ed, likes to think of himself as a free and well-educated person. He lives in Oregon where he listens to jazz and indulges in all manner of degeneracy. On occasion he can be coerced into writing for others. Edward spends a surprising amount of time in the gym and urges others to try to do the same.

• • • •

V.R. LEAVITT grew up in Northern Virginia but is happy to call Orlando, Florida her home since 2010. Being a theme park enthusiast, Orlando is a good fit. When she's not writing, she's shooing cats off her desk, collecting vinyl, going to her daughter's band concerts, and watching movies. She is also the co-founder of WhirlWhirl Publishing along with David J. Knight. You can get in touch with her at https://www.facebook.com/vrleavittauthor

. . . .

CHRISTOPH BRUCE is an academic and a writer, but mostly views himself as a petty intellectual. A graduate of the University of North Carolina at Charlotte, he has worked as a local public servant in Virginia and briefly as an instructor at Howard University in the District of Columbia. He currently resides in a small cabin in Hampshire County, West Virginia with a cat named Climacus and some stink bugs who keep getting into the cabin no matter how much caulking is applied. When not working, he spends his time trying to convince other folks to grow more mulberry and pawpaw trees.

. . . .

CHRISTOPHER B. OUTLAW is an Adjunct Lecturer of Philosophy at Northern Virginia Community College and the President of the Virginia Philosophical Association. He has a Master's in Philosophy from George Mason University. Outside of academia, he founded and facilitated a local reading group on the works of Soren Kierkegaard called "Kierkegaard on the Potomac" for several years until it found the sickness unto death and co-sponsors a Dungeons and Dragons Club at a local middle school. He is also a rather poor excuse for a handyman, and fails to meet his fiancé's expectations on woodworking projects. He is a United States Navy veteran.

Acknowledgements

First and foremost, I would like to extend my gratitude to my friends and family. I could not have completed this book without the lifetime of support and experiences you have afforded me.

The contributors, authors, artists, and editors of *Nose Candy* were rockstars. Quite frankly, you all needed to be to get me past my learning curve.

I would also like to thank the fine people who chose not to be contributors on the finished *Nose Candy* project. Some of you had reasons for not wanting to join the project and others were unable to finish, but all of you provided me with knowledge that allowed me to build a better version of *Nose Candy* than I could have ever done without you.

Outro

Dear Brave Soul,

Congrats, you did it! Let it be known that you can handle a lot of *Nose Candy*. Fear thee not, we'll let your family and co-workers know.

I hope that you enjoyed everything that our contributors had to offer. If not, please, let me know who you didn't like. I'll get rid of them.

All of the contributors to this anthology are at various stages in their creative careers, but most have already produced other works or will be releasing something very soon. I invite you to take another look at their bios, and see if you can find other works of theirs to love.

Please, keep your eyes out for *An Outlaw Entitlement - Short Story Anthology Volume 2*. It will be out next year. We should have a good mix of some returning contributors with some new ones as well. I can't wait to tell them all what their new title will be.

Kisses.

Christopher B. Outlaw

Managing Editor

Guy who has figured out the word count.